GW00600992

NeW Fic ion

WORKINGS OF FATE

Edited by

Kelly Oliver

First published in Great Britain in 2004 by
NEW FICTION
Remus House,
Coltsfoot Drive,
Peterborough, PE2 9JX
Telephone (01733) 898101
Fax (01733) 313524

All Rights Reserved

Copyright Contributors 2004

SB ISBN 1 85929 108 2

FOREWORD

When 'New Fiction' ceased publishing there was much wailing and gnashing of teeth, the showcase for the short story had offered an opportunity for practitioners of the craft to demonstrate their talent.

Phoenix-like from the ashes, 'New Fiction' has risen with the sole purpose of bringing forth new and exciting short stories from new and exciting writers.

The art of the short story writer has been practised from ancient days, with many gifted writers producing small, but hauntingly memorable stories that linger in the imagination.

I believe this selection of stories will leave echoes in your mind for many days. Read on and enjoy the pleasure of that most perfect form of literature, the short story.

Parvus Est Bellus.

CONTENTS

Wicked Rekindling	F D Gunn	1
The Beautiful Sand	Mark Cleaver	7
A Special Christmas Promise	Ann Blair	13
Petula Accidentally	J G Williams	18
Family Ties	Lynsey Tocker	22
The Beekeeper	Marc Shemmans	27
The Black And White Photograph	Emma Lockyer	33
Long Tail	Ian W Robinson	37
An Artistic Solution	Kathleen Townsley	43
The Visitation	Peter Jennison	48
Fear	Valerie E Pope	52
Murder, Suicide, Or?	Ron Bird	56
Timeslip	David Spanton	62
The Garden Gate	M C Jones	65
Albert's House	Sam McLean	68
Death Comes Like A Thief In The Night - Twice?	Gerard Allardyce	73
Will Cinders	Joyce Walker	77
Martha	Phyllis Spooner	82
All About Me	Lyndsay Cox	86
Hallowe'en Capers	Cynthia Davis	92
The Interview	Pearl Cannon	96
Stepping Stones	T G Bloodworth	101
Moving Day	Julie Weatleans	103

WICKED REKINDLING
F D Gunn

'Good morning listeners, you're waking up to the sounds of 'Lost Loves Rekindled', it's Sunday 18th of October, 8am, I'm Derek Smart playing the songs you fell in lurve to.'

This is the life; Diane revelled in the luxury of a lazy day. She could hear her beloved husband Edward clattering about in the kitchen, making her breakfast. Yes it was a good man she had married twenty-two years ago. She'd been incredibly lucky to find him.

Every Sunday, with a few exceptions she lazed in bed listening to slushy love songs on the radio while Edward brought her his speciality, with few exceptions, an omelette. Granted she'd once mentioned she liked them in '83 and had been 'enjoying' them ever since! He always varied the fillings; bless him, so she really had little cause to complain.

'Oh my darlin' you look wonderful tonight' she hummed, pulling the bedclothes under her chin, shivering slightly and sniffing the cold air and distinctive smell of . . . yes, omelette flying.

'You are listening to Lost Loves Rekindled, that was Eric Clapton with Wonderful Tonight, now to your letters.'

This was Diane's favourite part of the show, where listeners could write in with their stories of love, past and present or surprise people with messages and declarations of love. She often wondered if she should write in, express her love for her hero, 'Omelette Man' but she never did.

'I have a long letter here from Margaret Bryce.'

Diane gasped, surely not Maggie Maggie, that Maggie, *the* Maggie! Her evil twin, well step-sister.

Derek continued, 'I won't read it all, but briefly Maggie claims she met her first love Edward Vickers over thirty years ago.'

Diane gasped, it *was* her! That Maggie was back!

Diane abruptly sat up, fully conscious and rudely awakened from her cosy haze.

Derek went on, 'Margaret says Eddie was her boyfriend when she was just 19, they were practically joined at the hip for months when he told her he had joined the Royal Navy as a mechanical engineer and had been posted overseas.'

Hmph, her boyfriend, *my* husband!

Derek went on, 'Eddie left with promises of regular letters. After 8 months without replies to her own letters, Margaret, assuming he'd met someone else, gave up. She then met and married Gary.'

'Good, you've got your man Maggie, leave mine alone!'

'Unfortunately the marriage lasted only 4 months before Margaret admitted to herself that Gary was not 'the one'.'

Feeling slightly threatened now Diane turned down the volume fearing that Edward could hear.

'Now on her own, following a second failed marriage Margaret would like to make contact with Eddie.'

I bet she does! Diane's blood pressure high-jumped.

'So if you're out there Eddie get in touch, even if it's just to say hi and that you're happily married.'

This was too much, Diane leapt out of bed, he *is* happily married, has been for twenty-two years! Furiously she pummelled the pillows and shook the life out of the sheets.

She jumped guiltily as she heard Edward calling, 'Morning Sweetheart.' Swiftly she snapped off the nasty radio, pulled on her old bathrobe and threw herself on the newly made bed, pretending to read, grabbed a dog-eared magazine and feigned great interest in an article on pantyhose.

'How's my girl?'

She laughed, aged 53, a soon to be great-aunt, Diane hardly felt girlish, even less so now that she felt she had competition for Edward's attention. Diane tried to tell herself she was being ridiculous. It was after all *her*, he was cooking omelettes for, with varying fillings no less!

After he left the room she put the radio back on and listened to George Michael singing, 'Baby, I'm Your Man,' before jotting down the contact address.

That afternoon after Diane had waved Edward off to golf, she sat down at their new home computer to write to Lost Loves Rekindled posing as Yvette, Eddie's fictitious widow.

It was less than a fortnight since their nephew Michael had patiently explained the basics of this contraption.

Diane wished she hadn't found the whole thing so yawn worthy and maybe now she wouldn't be staring blankly at a blank screen.

After ages of clicking OK messages, she decided she felt far from OK and with disgust switched off the 'damn thing'. *E-mail was for young things*, she decided, *not ancient ole pre-great-aunties like her*, she thought.

Hand-written letter triumphantly in her hand Diane strode to the post-box, pausing only briefly to chat to neighbours as she went.

Briefly she wondered if she could be prosecuted for deception? Was she tempting fate? Oh well, too late now, she sighed, completing her delivery. As she strolled home through the streets Diane reminisced times spent with her Maggie. The Maggie.

Two years her junior, Maggie was considered the more beautiful of the two young girls. With her exotic dark looks and shiny black hair. Maggie delighted in winning much male attention.

Diane, forever in her shadow, was thought to be the more intelligent and was certainly more studious. Unruly blonde frizz surrounded a pretty enough face but it drew few second glances.

Diane of course aspired to university, while Maggie had more glamorous ideas of becoming a air hostess, although in actual fact she became a make-up consultant in a department store.

As Diane embarked on her long bus trip to Aberdeen University, she promised Maggie they could keep up their friendship through letters, and she would visit on holidays.

For some months the girls wrote letters, Diane describing her new life as a student and Maggie enthusing over the new brand of mascara, that really made your eyelashes longer.

Although they had little in common, Diane enjoyed hearing Maggie's adventures. Her letters made light and humorous reading. After an hour trying to study the delights of organic chemistry, mascara tales were just what she needed! She couldn't help envying Maggie her frivolous life of face packs, lipsticks and boys.

Both girls were looking forward to the Christmas holidays when they would see each other again.

Reaching home Diane sighed wondering how different her life would have been had she returned that Christmas?

Unexpectedly, Diane's mum and her stepfather had separated that year, leaving Diane to deck the university halls alone, while her parents decided who got what and who lived where.

Both girls were quite unhappy, but agreed it could be for the best as Diane had revision to do and Maggie was busy with her new boyfriend Edward, mascara, etc.

Lovely smells wafted from the kitchen as Diane arrived home. She had just enough time for a quick cup of tea before Edward came home from golf in search of his Sunday roast dinner.

Ah yes, Diane remembered how Eddie's appearance marked the end of their friendship. As Maggie grew more besotted her letter writing became more infrequent.

'Good game love?' she dutifully asked over roast beef that evening.

'Great,' he enthused.

'Lovely weather too, mmm lovely dinner, what's for dessert?'

Diane wondered what Edward would say if he knew how she had spent the day. Thank goodness for the distraction of frozen cheesecake!

The radio show phoned mid-morning on Thursday. Maggie had expressed an interest in meeting her and given them her phone number to pass on to the fictitious 'Yvette'.

Diane sat staring at the number before her. She could either use it or lose it. What could be gained from seeing this woman, what was to lose?

Nervously she punched in the numbers, she almost hung up before it was answered.

'Hello?' It was Maggie.

After a few deep breaths, Diane was able to reply, 'Hello, is that Maggie Bryce? This is Yvette Vickers, Edward's widow, the radio station gave me your number.'

'Yes Diane, I was hoping you'd call, I was sorry to hear about your loss.' Diane felt guilt about lying to her old companion. But her stepsister was not to be trusted with other people's men, her's in particular!

The two women agreed to meet up the following week in a seaside cafe. That week seemed endless, as Diane counted down the days and then the minutes until their meeting.

Diane recalled the many occasions the pair, as young girls had enjoyed amiable chats over huge mugs of creamy hot chocolate and sugary doughnuts in similar cafes.

Now decades later she prepared herself for a very different meeting with Maggie.

Entering the cafe Diane looked around and immediately located Maggie. The Maggie, her Maggie, her stepsister hadn't changed.

Praying for courage as she approached the table. Diane knew she had some explaining to do. And apologies to make, she reluctantly conceded.

'Hello Diane, or should I say Yvette? How are you?' Maggie did not seem surprised or pleased to see her.

Knees failing her, Diane managed to seat herself across from Maggie.

'I had a phone call from a ghost this week.'

Edward's golf partner had heard the radio show.

At this revelation Edward walked in.

'I gather you have both met?' he glared angrily at Diane.

'Perhaps you would care to explain these,' he spat as he dumped a bundle of old letters on the table. Letters addressed 'To my darling Maggie'.

'Emmm,' Diane spluttered, unable to speak.

A young waitress hovering awkwardly nearby noted the silence and approached the table.

'Are you ready to order?' she whispered. No response.

After some time Edward said, 'Not yet, thanks.' The girl moved away.

'An explanation, now!' Edward bellowed. Diane had never known him to be so angry.

'No Eddie, allow me, I think I can explain the actions of your lovely wife, my favourite sister.'

Maggie outlined the situation while Diane shamefully listened and Edward grew more irate.

When Diane's mother and Maggie's father separated, Diane and her mother remained in the family home while Maggie and her father moved away. Jealous of her younger sister's life, Diane took it upon herself to direct fate, read and return Edward's letters. Thus both lovers thought the other had lost interest.

Having heard enough Edward stormed out.

Neither woman spoke.

Eventually Maggie broke the silence, 'Why Diane? You were the intelligent one, doing so well, going places, why did you do it?'

Diane smiled, 'Don't you realise I had to do it for us? I missed you Maggie, Edward stole my best friend from me, and I wanted you back.'

Maggie sat in silence, stunned by the admissions.

Diane continued, 'Never did I expect to fall for Edward, I only wanted you to come home.'

On returning from the Navy, Edward attempting to find Maggie had visited her old address. Diane told him she had just moved home and had never heard of anyone called Maggie living there.

'So you just claimed the man *I* loved for yourself?' Maggie was furious.

'It wasn't like that,' Diane protested.

'Oh spare me the details, I don't want to know, all that I know is that your interfering behaviour has affected all of our lives for years, you robbed me of my true love and robbed my daughter of her father!'

Diane gasped.

'Yes Diane, I am here to get my man back. I always win in the end, you know.' Unfortunately she did.

THE BEAUTIFUL SAND
Mark Cleaver

'You promised me the sea.'
   'You always say that.'
   'We agreed.'
   He sighed. 'We did.'
   'It was the only thing that connected us.'
   'It wasn't the only thing.'
   'Yeah, I know. I meant . . . it was our 'thing'. It marked us out from the crowd.'
   Jonas put his hands on the steering wheel, 'ten-to-two', locked his arms at the elbow and pushed all the air out of his lungs. He stared long and hard at the tiny, thin strip of beach and the dark sea, running out to the horizon. He could see the water, unmoving, still like a pane of glass, a windscreen. The sea seemed to be holding its breath.
   'All those beaches we used to stand on,' she said, quietly.
   'It's so hard, these days. Now that you've left.' He paused, swallowing hard, thrusting one lip down hard onto the other. 'I loved you so much.'
   'You talk in the past tense.'
   He changed the subject. There were still things he couldn't say. He'd had these conversations with his wife before. Many times they had discussed the sand.
   How it would be wet or dry. How it would stretch for miles, a historical statement beneath their bare feet. All the piggy-back rides. All the candy floss. All the tiny, empty shells that they had collected, would wash in the caravan at the end of the day, and take back home.
   Jenny laughed, 'All those stupid sayings you had.'
   'They were true.'
   'All your mottos.'
   'And?'
   'The girls at work called you 'Hello Motto'.'
   'It didn't seem to bother you.'
   'What was that you used to say? Famous people who didn't figure in literature: one - Captain Ahab's wife'.'
   'Was Mrs Aesop just a fable?'
   'Yeah. That was another conversation-killer down the pub.'

Jonas watched as an old woman walked past, her dog tearing ahead of her on one of those long leads that you let out and reel in.

'I'm finding it hard to be positive.'

'I've been gone some time.'

'We had such great days. Standing on the beach, all the kids building sandcastles: day-trippers sunbathing at our feet, standing room only.'

'And I would shout: 'Where's the sea? You promised me the sea'.'

'I promised you so much.'

'You did.'

Jen touched his arm with the tips of her fingers, lightly, gently. Jonas looked down, away from the sand dunes, away from the line separating sea from sky, blue from aquamarine, the past from the future.

'I miss you so much.'

'It'll pass. You'll find someone else.'

'I don't want to find somebody. I want you. I only ever wanted you.'

Jonas began to cry. A silent cry, where the tears ran down your cheeks, but there was no other outward, visible sign of dejection. A tear dripped from his chin onto the car seat between his legs.

'You promised me the sea, I would shout above the roaring waves. Where . . . is . . . your . . . promise, I would shout, and you would reply?'

'My promise is my love . . .'

' . . . washed ashore,' Jen added.

Tears rolled down his cheeks, remembering, feeling the past creep up on him, cloak him like a comfort blanket. Jonas could see the sofa she would lie on.

'I felt so alone.'

'Alone as an imploding star.'

He was shocked. 'How do you . . . ?'

'You said it to me. Remember? Straight after Danny died?'

Jonas thought about his little son. The sea was out there. A line above and below the horizon. It had made no sense to stand in the sand, when there was the sea. The sea would cleanse her, bring her closer to him, until the tide took hold.

'We followed all our memories to the sea. Just as the counsellor suggested.'

'All grey and burnt. All yellow and green, like a watercolour.'

'It *was* a good promise,' said Jen, warmly.

Jonas smiled. 'Is this not my promise? The sea. Will we always be defined by the sea? Will we always be defined by Danny? He got sick, Jen. That was all.'

'He was so ill. I cried so much, that we couldn't do anything.'

'Nobody could do anything.'

'He was so scared. That look in his eyes, like he didn't know what was happening, and we kept telling him everything would be alright.'

'Nobody talked more than we did, Jen.'

'We couldn't save him.'

'The doctors couldn't save him.'

Jonas saw the staff watching them as they held their little son, wrapped and lifeless, his little head falling back over his right forearm, the tiny mouth slumping open. He could see Jen in her black top, bursting into tears like a spring fountain, the water flying through the fingers of her hands as she brought them up to her mouth.

Jonas could see, beyond the beach and the sea, his wife's eyes red and sore from the anguish and the pain. He could see her double up in intense agony and roll into a ball on the floor of the hospital room. Staff helped her into a chair, mindful that he wouldn't let anybody touch his son. Jonas held him until Jen stopped crying, and then he handed his son to his wife.

'You were a stranger to me then,' he added.

His wife didn't answer.

'We used to laugh so much,' she said, finally. 'We used to watch the seagulls dive-bomb us. Watch the boats leave the harbours. We used to sit for hours just watching, and talking.'

'You were the only woman I ever met that made me realise that an individual has a soulmate out there. Somebody that completes that circle.'

'Even with stupid sayings.'

'They never bothered you way back when.'

'What was it you said: 'A man who works twice as fast as anybody else, will never be short of work'.'

'That's true.'

Jen laughed. 'Still the same old Jonas; still sulking.'

The car was silent. Jonas stared at a man and woman walking their dog. It was early evening and the sun was setting behind them, casting an eerie, bright orange glow over the sea, quiet and benevolent in the distance.

The man threw a piece of wood into the air. The Labrador loped after it.

'Before Danny was born; this was our time of day.'

'Remember all those sunsets we used to stay out for?'

'Hundreds. Even if it was behind us. We'd stay on the beach, huddled together . . .'

' . . . hugging . . .'

'Whispering sweet nothings to each other . . .'

'And stupid sayings -'

'They weren't stupid,' he protested.

'How could we be so happy, but then not happy?'

There was too much silence in the car, now. Jonas could sense his wife crying, even if he couldn't bring himself to turn and look. He didn't like the silence: it was cold and intimidating, like meeting a gang of thugs in the dark. Silence had a hard edge to it, one that warmth rounded, moulded, caressed.

Tears sprang to his eyes, again.

'We got married on the sand,' he said, the words sticking in his throat.

The tears stung his already salty cheeks, like hailstones being spat at him from dark clouds of lips. 'The beautiful sand.'

Jen smiled. 'It was, truthfully, a great day. A great idea; to write 'The Beautiful Sand' on all the wedding invitations.'

'It was your idea.'

'I was only joking. But you went and did it, created the whole thing. Mum and Dad's face. It was a picture.'

'And your mate Maggie sent hers back in an envelope marked -'

'Dear 'Motto-Man'.'

Jen laughed, a bright, piercing cry of delight from the clearness of her shrewd and pleasant mind. Brightness in her eyes. He always remembered her smile in her eyes, the darkness and lustre of warm, melting chocolate, lit from behind with the light of a thousand stars.

Jen always reminded him of Raphael's 'Sistine Madonna'. The supremely dignified figure of the Virgin, whose veil swells with an invisible wind, carries the Child as she walks towards the viewer upon a soft, white cloud. The whole scene is illuminated by a cold, clear light, most intense behind the head of the Virgin, like an impalpable halo. Jen would never understand any of this, until he took her to Dresden one summer to see the famous altarpiece.

Jonas always said that Raphael's 'Madonnas' were characterised by their grace, sweetness and modesty, qualities which were emphasised by their softened features and gently lowered eyelids. Lost in reverie, they would usually gaze quietly and tenderly downwards.

Most of *Jen's* mates would tell her that they were the most unmatched couple they had *ever* met, but none of them truly understood where they *had* met; in each other's eyes, in each other's souls.

Jen was always sure of this. They could laugh together, and that was all that mattered, she used to say.

'I love you Jonas, I always will. Our love will always connect us.'

'My heart aches for you. Every night it keeps me awake, Jen. It hurts so much without you.'

Everything seemed so mixed up, so impermanent, so terrifying, as if his whole existence had become an ocean of movement, of winds and tides, of swirling currents and cold sea spray.

'Is this not my promise?'

'You promised me the sea, Jonas. I followed you, after Danny died. And I was so proud to follow you.'

Jonas began to scream.

'Did I not promise you the sea?'

'Don't cry. Please don't cry. I can't come back, honey. I can't . . . come . . . back.'

'I trusted you.'

'I trusted you, too.'

'I *trusted* you not to leave me. I was so angry, Jen. It was so selfish. To go like that.'

'I will always love you, Jonas. Wherever you go, I will always love you.'

'Soooo,' he screamed, locking his arms at the elbows once more, pushing the steering wheel into the dashboard and out of the car, through the engine and onto the sand. It wouldn't budge, and he struggled, his face reddening with terror and anxiety. Jonas felt the terror of being on his own. The anguish of not being with his wife.

'I looked down at you, when they pulled you from the sea. When they'd left me with you, and your eyes . . . were closed . . . and they let me hold you, but you were so cold . . . and I couldn't stop crying . . . and you were so beautiful . . . but you wouldn't breathe for me . . . you weren't breathing, and . . . just everything faded from view . . . the sounds on the beach . . . the noise of the sand . . . and you just lay there in my arms . . . and I couldn't stop myself crying and the all the tears fell onto your wet hair . . . but your lips . . . your lips were so dark and soft, and I kissed your lips . . . and I stroked your hair forever . . . but I couldn't do anything . . . you were gone. You were gone, Jen. The most beautiful woman I ever met . . . my other half . . .'

Jen placed her cold hand on his arm. Jonas jumped a mile, moved away from her touch, edged closer towards his door.

'Just tell me why you did it. Before you go?'

'I couldn't go on. I couldn't look at you, anymore.'

'Why? Why me?'

'Because every time I looked at you, I saw Danny. And I couldn't do that, anymore.'

Jonas began to smash the palms of his hands on the steering wheel. His tears fell into his lap. His chest hurt so much that he held his sides, and his body was so doubled up he had to rest his forehead on the middle of the steering wheel.

'Jen . . .'

'I love you with all my heart,' she whispered, gently kissing the side of his head. 'Please forgive me.'

Jonas heard the words ebb away into the evening twilight. He felt his wife leave his side, as dusk enveloped the sea. He heard a car door slam shut. He saw the sun set through a watery film.

She was gone.

But the sea remained. Even as the tides come and go, so the sea remains. Jen was gone, like the tide.

A Special Christmas Promise
Ann Blair

It had been a year since Lance had left and Adele missed him almost
more than she could bear. She'd feared all along that one day he would
go. He was too young and too handsome to stay married to a woman
twelve years his senior, even if Adele didn't look her age. At forty-five
she still turned heads. A tall elegant, statuesque woman, whose chestnut
hair showed no sign of grey, and whose violet coloured eyes sparkled
with an exuberance for living.

Adele's charm, good humour and easy grace won her many friends
and they had helped her get over the death of her first husband, ten
years ago. Adele had been happy with John, who had left her well
provided for, and she vowed she wouldn't marry again, until Lance
exploded into her life. He was so different from her quiet, staid, first
husband. Lance was exciting and dangerous, a good-looking, sexy
young man, who had stolen Adele's heart completely. She had fallen in
love at first sight and wanted him more than anything else in the world.
Lance made Adele feel young and desirable, he was all of her fantasies
rolled into one. She was lost and no one could save her. Lance's touch
set her on fire, his lips tantalised and teased her, and his hands were
pure magic when he played her body like a finely tuned instrument.
Lance fulfilled Adele completely. For the first time in her life she was
driven by pure passion and enjoyed sex more than she had previously
thought possible. Lance knew exactly how to please her and, as her
confidence grew, he taught Adele how to please him too. Each time
they made love it was like taking an amazing journey, when they would
soar to the stars in the primeval act as old as time and creation. Their
bodies were made for each other, their sex life incredible, and to the
surprise and disapproval of most of her friends, Adele married Lance
just three months after she met him.

For two years Adele was gloriously happy. She was a wealthy
woman and liked nothing better than indulging her younger husband,
and encouraging Lance to write the novel, he was convinced would be a
best seller. But last Christmas Eve everything had fallen apart. Lance's
book had been rejected and he was sullen and depressed. Adele had
tried to jolly him out of it, but that only made things worse. He refused
to go to the dinner party they'd been invited to and, after a furious row,

Lance stormed out of the penthouse flat they shared. Adele hadn't heard a word from him since and the hope she'd nurtured had finally died with the approach of this year's festive season.

Adele didn't want to spend Christmas alone, but she couldn't face accepting any of the many invitations she'd received from her well-meaning friends. Adele needed to be with strangers. To be completely anonymous, to blend in with people who knew nothing about her, or how foolish she'd been in marrying a younger man who didn't love her. By going away Adele had avoided hurting her friends' feelings, and four days of being waited on hand and foot was just what the doctor ordered. The only problem was Adele couldn't blank out the thoughts or the memories that still haunted her. She knew she would never get over Lance; there was no one else like him and at times she felt her life had very little meaning. But Adele was determined not to wallow in self-pity or bear the brunt of her friends' sympathy this Christmas. She'd come away to escape all that and Adele's first impression of the destination she had chosen was very favourable indeed.

The old converted coach house was set in acres of woodland. A country retreat that offered luxury accommodation for those who could afford it. The friendly, efficient staff made Adele feel very welcome and the room she had booked turned out to be delightful. After unpacking her case, Adele showered and changed into a grape coloured chiffon pantsuit, ready to attend a champagne reception in the lounge. When she went downstairs she noticed that most of the other residents seemed to know each other, and that they were all quite elderly. This was not quite what Adele had expected. She had hoped that there would have been a few people nearer her own age, but it was too late now to change her mind. Howard, the very smart young manager, welcomed everyone to the hotel while his staff served the champagne, and then he came over to sit by Adele.

'I do hope you'll enjoy your stay.' He smiled pleasantly. 'We usually have quite a few people who come here alone at Christmas. But this year there is only yourself and one gentleman guest, who will be arriving later. I thought that perhaps the two of you could share a table in the restaurant.'

'Of course,' Adele replied graciously, thinking it would be preferable to eating alone for the entire holiday.

The Christmas Eve dinner was delicious, but there was still no sign of the missing guest when the meal was finally over. Howard was very attentive but Adele was beginning to regret leaving her friends at this time of year. She had never felt so lonely as she made her way to the bar and forcing a smile to her lips ordered a brandy. Sitting down at a corner table Adele tried to relax wishing she had someone to talk to. He came into the bar a few minutes later, a tall fair-haired young man and Adele's heart skipped a beat. Their eyes met and he smiled and she had difficulty breathing. When he came over and asked if he could join her Adele nodded wordlessly. She was inwardly trembling when he took a seat by her side, it was happening again and she couldn't control it. His smoky, grey eyes held her mesmerised until he asked, 'Why did you choose this place to spend Christmas?'

'I don't really know. I needed to get away and I thought there would be more people on their own,' Adele replied hesitantly.

'So did I,' he agreed, 'but we'll just have to make the best of it, that's if you want to of course?'

Adele nodded again, wishing he wasn't having such a devastating effect on her, and cursing herself for being so weak. They sat for a while in silence, observing the other guests who were quietly enjoying themselves. He replenished Adele's drink without asking and then said very softly, 'Why does such a lovely woman look so sad this evening?'

'Because a year ago tonight my husband left me,' she replied honestly.

'Why did he do that?' he asked thoughtfully.

'Probably because I'm twelve years older than he is,' Adele said a little bitterly.

'Surely that couldn't have been the reason. I think you are absolutely gorgeous, any man would be proud to be with you.'

Adele glanced up and saw the sincerity in his sensuous eyes, and smiled at him gratefully before she replied. 'I loved him very much. I wanted to give him everything, but obviously that wasn't enough.'

'Perhaps he felt smothered and had to prove himself. He could even have thought he wasn't worthy of you.'

Adele smiled again and when she saw the expression in his beautiful eyes she felt her insides churn. He was attracted to her, of that she had no doubt, but she wasn't going to make the same mistake again in a hurry.

'How about we both forget all our problems for the next few days?'
he continued, 'let's just live for now and enjoy each other's company
without worrying about the future.'

Adele nodded in agreement; under the circumstances she had very
little choice. But she wished she didn't feel so vulnerable and afraid of
being hurt again. She leant over to pick up her drink at the same time he
did; and for a moment his lips brushed against hers. He tried to deepen
the kiss but Adele drew away quickly.

'Don't, the others will see us.'

'I very much doubt that,' he laughed gently, 'most of them are in
their dotage.'

'Don't be cruel,' Adele chided, trying to block out the sensations his
brief kiss had evoked.

Then she tensed as he whispered, 'Come to bed with me. I want you
like crazy and unless I'm mistaken you want me too.'

Adele shook her head firmly, 'That is the drink talking. I don't want
either of us to do anything we'll regret in the morning.'

'I most certainly wouldn't regret it.' He shrugged but to Adele's
relief didn't push any further.

At midnight he wished her a happy Christmas and kissed her
chastely before Adele retired to her room. Her thoughts were in turmoil,
she hadn't felt like this since Lance had left and she wasn't sure what
Christmas Day would bring; but now she was excited at the prospect.
Surprisingly Adele fell asleep as soon as her head touched the pillow.
The dye was cast, he had to be here for a reason and she was content to
let fate take its course.

Adele's heart fluttered wildly when he came down to breakfast. His
easy smile completely won her over; she knew she was risking making
a fool of herself but Adele no longer cared. In the cold light of day she
knew how much she wanted him; and she was now ready to surrender if
he asked her again. It was Christmas and Adele wanted to be loved. She
longed for a man's arms around her, to be kissed until she was
senseless. They were both lonely so why not give in to the inevitable?

They joined in the morning's festivities and then went for a stroll,
after eating too much Christmas lunch. The weather was pleasant and
he was a wonderful companion. They talked about trivialities, nothing
too deep or too personal. He made her laugh with his quick wit and
made her feel special. The chemistry between them was electric. The air

almost sizzled when he looked at her in a certain way; and yet he made her feel safe and protected. Even if it proved to be only for a few days, Adele was happy again. He put his arm lightly around her shoulders as they walked back to the hotel and his eyes were full of promise when he took her hand into his. Adele willingly let him lead her to the wide staircase behind the reception desk. Neither spoke as they climbed the stairs, but both of them knew there was no turning back.

Locked in his powerful arms Adele journeyed to Heaven and back. It was even better than she'd remembered; and when at last they were both satisfied she gazed over at him lovingly.

'How did you know I would be here?' she asked softly.

'I have my ways,' he smiled and held her very closely.

'But why did you wait so long?'

'I had to get this published,' he replied reaching over to retrieve a hardbacked book from the bedside table. 'It took time to find the right publisher, but my agent is about to sell the film rights and I will be able to look after you the way I've always wanted to. And prove to your friends once and for all that I didn't marry you for your money. I love you Adele, I always have and I always will.'

'And I love you too Lance,' she whispered.

'Happy Christmas darling,' he sighed, 'I promise I'll never leave you again. Whatever happens in the future I'll always be here by your side. My life was hell without the woman I love. The one who captured my heart and made my life complete.'

PETULA ACCIDENTALLY
J G Williams

It was another energy draining day. When nothing went right, all I needed was sleep, good old forget-your-troubles sleep. But do you know I can't remember if I did sleep. What I remember is most bizarre.

Brown envelopes poured in through my letterbox scattering onto the floor like confetti. Just the sight of those envelopes set my stomach churning. Two months before this day I had no money worries. I had a reasonable job, a boring job, but a job nonetheless. The only problem was I resented being treated like the office skivvy. I had more qualifications than the whole lot of them put together. It was always, type this, fetch that, make a brew. I always managed to control my temper, even if I did think evil thoughts. Like the day I imagined hanging Mr Osgood by his nuts with cheese wire through the office window. Though I knew that not one of them so-called work colleagues would even notice if I fell off the face of the earth. Anyway, I think that's what I did . . . fall off the face of the earth.

It must have been Wednesday; I *hate* Wednesdays. My in-tray was overflowing, the coffee machine was on the blink and I had filled myself full of caffeine to keep up with my workload. I could feel my head buzzing, just before I was thrown out of the office by two skinny security guards who thought they were the answer to Phil and Grant Mitchell. It must have been that last coffee; the word *coffee* just etched itself to my brain, vivid red in colour and boiling hot. Then a jumped up jerk called Jeremy called me Petuliar Peculiar, I just flipped. I went downstairs in the lift and ordered the office fire bucket to be filled with coffee from Mary's coffee bar. Mary was out and the dumb bimbo didn't ask any questions, she just did as I asked and took my money. I struggled back to the office, spilling some of the hot liquid. But I was on a mission, my head thumped with anticipation. I stood outside the office door for a few minutes and head them making fun of me. Then, shaking, I opened the door and shouted, '*coffeeeeee*'. Then I proceeded to throw the whole bucketful over them. The shocked look on their faces sent me into fits of laughter. The screams and howls of scolded bodies and rockets of exploding computers gave me the utmost satisfaction until . . . Mr Osgood 'the big boss' emerged from his office with a face as red as the burned bodies wriggling on the floor. I swear I could see steam pouring from every orifice on his body.

Anyway, I was prescribed some kind of new tranquilliser. Because they said I was suffering from the showed signs of psychosis or anxiety or depression, or maybe complete madness. I strongly disagreed with *that* diagnosis. So like a good girl I took my pills and went to bed. I remember waking up a few times during the night, I may have took some more pills, but they made me feel all floaty and nice. Soon I drifted and started on a journey of incredible dreams.

Firstly, I met my brother: this was *news to me.* He introduced himself, 'I am your brother from the last century, we have a lot of work to do before we say goodbye.' I never doubted his word and went with him. This was the start of my journey.

First I had to fly. This was hard, I have a fear of heights and it was the beginning of winter. So up we went my brother and I, up to the rooftop. He held my hand and away we went, right up into the clouds. I couldn't resist breaking off a piece of cloud just to have a taste. It felt cold to the touch and fizzed like sherbet on my tongue then it melted away to water. My body ached from the physical exertion. My brother said this was normal and that I would have to learn to walk through objects.

'You must be having a laugh,' I said. But his face was as serious as a mask. Wood seemed much easier than brick. I pushed my hand into the trunk of an old oak tree, then my arm, half my body then my legs and head. Once out the other side I found I had splinters everywhere, even in places where doctors blush to look. Heard the saying *banging your head against a brick wall*? That's exactly what it's like.

'Don't worry it's only breeze blocks,' my brother said. I had bumps, cuts and grazes all over and spent three days in bed. The angels were very kind, musical when they spoke, radiating a warm glowing light. They said not everyone could see them, only those chosen.

So they allotted me a car. I can't drive but I can drive this one. You see the wheels are off the ground. I had to pick up four passengers, I was told that I would know who they were, and funnily enough I did. They all had this luminous glow about them. The first one, a girl of about twenty, stood shrouded in a golden light at a bus stop. She smiled but try as I might I couldn't *drag* a conversation out of her. The other three, all men, were waiting on the motorway of all places. Not on the hard shoulder mind you, but the middle lane! I felt pins and needles each time a car went through us, and those *juggernauts!* Just don't ask how I am still in one piece. They climbed into the car, no words, just a smile. I ranted on about the traffic but none of them took any notice, well it wasn't the first time I had been ignored. I dropped them off somewhere near the moon, a shuttle took them from there, and I had to go off on other business. My brother took over the wheel and we headed off to see what damage was being done to the ozone layer. High above we looked down, it's a pretty blue filter above the earth. It looked azure in most places but the holes spoiled the smoothness. I wondered whether we could knit it back together? But that would be defeating the object I was told. Whatever that meant. So we sat on a passing meteor and watched the fuel emissions being sucked through the holes. I guessed it was Bonfire Night. I could smell the burning rubber of used car tyres. The smog completely obscured the azure blue, even the moon developed a chesty cough. I wondered about global warming, and imagined the earth red beneath me, burned up by the rays of the sun. A group of passing angels told me to return home before dawn and await further instructions. This I did. but someone had moved into my bed!

She didn't speak either, so I climbed in bed beside her. After all it was *my* bed. I closed my eyes and dreamed of a long escalating stairway, I tried to get on but each time I stopped on the bottom step. I feel the months are flying by.

I awoke this morning to more brown envelopes, I don't intend to open them. It's funny how the house seems so dusty and I've no idea where all the cobwebs have come from. I can walk through the walls now without pain. For fun I stand in the middle of the wall so I can see both rooms at once. *That* woman is still asleep in my bed; she must be exhausted. My brother called to say he was leaving, I asked if I could leave too but he said I had to pay penance and to await instructions.
I said, 'All this over a spot of coffee?'
He replied, 'It has nothing to do with that.' He's gone now and I'm alone again . . . except for that *woman*, and some company she is!

I've been busy crocheting some fine blue thread to mend the holes in the sky. It's hard to do because the thread is so light it floats. The living room is full of it now, reams and reams of it. Oh yes, the *woman* in my bed has gone, some men in uniform took her. They also took *my* bottles of pills; I don't know why, they didn't belong to *her*. Hey my windows have been boarded up! I shouted for ages for them to stop but they took no notice of me. Anyway I can walk through them if the fancy takes me. Good news, no more brown envelopes, that makes me smile. Ouch! A golden envelope has passed through the ceiling and hit me on the nose. I must roll up my crocheting and get ready for embarkation. Just in time . . . because those builders are tearing my kitchen apart and there's only so much of 'builder's bum' I can take!

At last here it is the golden stairway. If they could see me now, all those stuffed shirts at the office. They said I would never be employed by anyone again. Ha! Ha! . . . Wrong. I think I must be a very special person because only a special person would be chosen to repair the sky.

FAMILY TIES
Lynsey Tocker

It was already warm. The Mediterranean air was close, even at six in the morning. The sun was up, the waves were gentle and the beach was deserted apart from one figure in the distance walking along the beach with his dog enjoying the spray as he ran along the ocean shore.

That feeling of being on vacation was around. There wasn't any urgency to abide by times or timetables, meetings or targets. Just that early morning feeling of pleasure. A new day to live.

Paul stood by the hotel window looking out onto the ocean, the beach, the empty sunbeds and the still water in the pool below. His partner Jane, asleep in the bed a few metres away oblivious to his thoughts. In the room next door his daughter Annabelle was sleeping after a late night out with the family. She kept up well for a two-year old. She'd probably be asleep for at least another hour.

In the hotel room next door was his parents. Besides them were his sister and her husband. His younger sister Sarah was expecting her first baby. The pregnancy and heat of July weren't mixing well. Jane and Sarah spent most of the days under the large sun umbrellas with Annabelle. Discussing pregnancy, labour and motherhood, as Jane would kindly run through all the details to Paul as they got ready on an evening for dinner.

Then on the floor above was Paul's older brother and his girlfriend Nicola. They had no children, they were on a different floor and a different level altogether when it came to the traditional ways of their family's life. They'd been together almost two years but had no plans to marry. Nicola wasn't the marrying sort she'd told Paul one evening when they first got to know one another. His brother Simon was the break away in the family you could say. He'd always done things differently to his brother, sister and his parents. But it was his girlfriend Nicola who was really different in Paul's eyes.

Nicola bought about a different style of living. She had both a lovely, caring manner but came with excitement and adventure too. She almost lived on the edge and had this glow about her that attracted people. His parents loved her. Jane and Sarah thought she was great fun, though at times there was almost a hint of jealousy in their eyes. She seemed to have it all, while they had the expected.

Paul first met Nicola at a barbecue. His brother had said he was bringing along his new girlfriend. They'd been together three months. Paul was waiting at the barbecue for Jane's hamburger when a sweet young voice from behind said, 'Excuse me, could you tell me where the kitchen is?'

Paul turned round and was faced by deep brown eyes and long chestnut coloured hair. Until that moment, Jane had been the most beautiful woman in his life, along with his precious daughter Annabelle of course. But who was this? Paul was speechless and he couldn't help but just look in amazement at this woman. Nicola just smiled. The moment was disturbed when Simon came across shouting, 'There you are Babe. Chatting up my brother already!' Paul looked down to the ground and Nicola lent forward and kissed Simon.

'I see you two have already met. I was just going to introduce you.'

'No we haven't I was just getting Jane's food and . . .' Paul realised he didn't know this beautiful woman's name.

'Well let me introduce you. Paul this is Nicola my girlfriend who I've been telling you about, and Nicola this is my brother. He's married to Jane and that's their little daughter in the pram over there. She's so cute; little Annabelle.'

Nicola put out her hand to Paul. 'Nice to meet you Paul.'

Wasn't that meant to be my job? Paul thought, *aren't I meant to be the confident male?*

'Hi, nice to meet you. The kitchen's round the corner and to your left by the way.' That was all he could manage to say. 'Excuse me I have to get back to Jane.'

From that moment on something changed inside of Paul. He thought he was happy and content with life, but as the months went on something seemed to be wrong. There seemed to be a gap in his life. A feeling that something was missing or out there that he hadn't caught.

Paul's family were close. They always had been. They did a lot together and shared many happy times. Christmas was always a big event in their parents' house. That first Christmas after the barbecue though wasn't the usual happy event for Paul. Well, in fact every family event or time spent with Nicola and his brother was more like an event to try and get out of. There was something about Nicola that Paul couldn't ignore or didn't want to. She was a breath of fresh air compared to the usual talk of weddings, babies and family life which until recently Paul had been content with, or so he believed. Jane and Paul did have their wilder days, when they first met about four years ago, but they seemed so distant now. Everything seemed so routine these days, planned out. Sex was mainly just on the to-do list. If Jane had enough energy after a week with Annabelle then she and Paul would spend an hour together in bed at the weekend. Followed by Annabelle coming in for a cuddle shortly afterwards.

Paul would pretend to listen over a pint when his brother would talk about his sexual activities with Nicola and how amazing she was.

'I'm telling you, marriage and kids just doesn't go with excitement and heat-of-the-moment stuff!'

Paul felt guilty as he did love Jane and he adored his daughter. But the more he got to know Nicola the more he felt he was missing out. What was worse though was when Paul knew Nicola felt that awkward pressure when they were together too.

The Christmas dinner table had been arranged. Paul was to sit opposite Nicola. As if it wasn't enough to be in the same room all day, he now had to sit looking at her in front of his family and while his brother sat on the opposite side of the table. They would catch each others stare and smiles from time to time. Paul was mesmerised by the way Nicola would wrap her hands around her coffee cup and play with the edge of the mug with her nails. Everything about her was so petite, neat and perfect. The red dress Nicola was wearing showed off her slimline figure. Her collar bone and shoulders were on display and just waiting to be kissed. Her long legs were hidden under the table, *thank God,* thought Paul.

Towards the end of Christmas dinner and with the wine bottles almost empty, Paul was about ready to get out of the room for some air. He leaned forward to pass a clean napkin to his sister when he felt someone's leg rub up to his knee. His eyes instantly looked at Nicola. She just smiled as she did in that innocent way. 'I'll clean away Mom and bring some more coffee in shall I?' Paul quickly went into the kitchen.

'I'll give him a hand, you go and see to Annabelle,' Nicola said to Jane.

Nicola walked into the kitchen and brushed past Paul as he stood at the sink looking out the window. She placed the empty glasses on the side. Nicola knew what she'd like to do, but she also cared for Paul's daughter and family. She liked Jane but didn't think she was right for Paul. However she wasn't going to start something that maybe Paul didn't want. After all he'd married her and seemed to pull off a pretty convincing performance of happiness in front of his family. She stood there for a moment before going to leave the room. As she did, Paul blocked her way with his arm. She looked up at him. 'Excuse me Paul I need to get by.' It wasn't just her beauty that captured Paul, it was everything about her. She wasn't like any of the women he knew. She reminded him of how he used to be when he was younger. When his life was excited and you never knew what the next day would bring. He'd loved the chats they'd had about so many things. He loved the way Nicola made him feel, but he hated not being able to go any further.

With his arm still blocking her way she looked into his eyes. There had been many moments like this where they had been within arms' reach of one another. Times when they'd been too close for comfort, times when one of them was going to give in to temptation. God knows they'd both dreamed about it. Maybe that's what they just needed. A one off moment of passion to put out the flames and then things could return to normal. Nicola could just be his future sister-in-law, they could manage to be in the same room without this burning desire for one another.

Nicola leaned forward and kissed Paul on the cheek as she heard his mother about to enter the kitchen. 'I know,' she whispered as she reluctantly drew back.

Jane turned over and stirred. Dreaming of something which made her smile. Maybe the birth of her next child. She'd already been asking Paul about a brother or sister for Annabelle.

Paul had once again gotten out of bed early to watch Nicola warm-up before her morning run. He looked down by the sunbeds and there she was stretching her toned body. Her hair shone in the sun and her body just made Paul feel weak. How could he have Nicola and not ruin his family? It wouldn't just be his marriage that would end. He was trapped in a dream while watching her, and a nightmare the rest of the time.

As she was about to start running down the hotel steps and on to the beach she turned and looked up at the 6th floor. Her heart ached knowing she'd have to spend another day sunbathing next to Simon and on the other side of her would be Paul. She hoped he'd offer to rub in some lotion again while Simon was asleep. To make it worse all the time smiling at Paul would be Jane, Sarah and little Annabelle. On the evening she'd only be able to read the messages from Paul's eyes as she entered the dining room in her new blue dress. The last evening of the holiday, and an announcement was to be made within the family?

Nicola smiled up to the 6th floor as she saw Paul leaning against the window. She'd wondered whether he'd be waiting one morning somewhere along where she ran and that he'd give in.

Her run would help clear her head from the thoughts of them together which she had while sleeping last night. She'd run, run to get away from the torment.

'Darling can you get Annabelle, she's calling for you.' Paul turned to his wife and away from the window. Nicola began her run along the water's edge . . .

THE BEEKEEPER
Marc Shemmans

Paul Williamson and Joan Pleasance made their way into the back garden where Stephen kept the bees. Stephen didn't speak or look at them. He stared across the garden to the distant woods.

They were both wearing the light coloured clothing that Paul's uncle always insisted they wear when they visited him. Apparently they had to avoid bright or dark colours because if they wore dark colours the bees might think they were bears and if they wore bright colours, the bees would be attracted to them as they would be to a bright coloured flower. Bee keeping was a very tricky business.

'I wonder what he wants?' whispered Joan.

'I don't know,' Paul whispered back.

They looked at Stephen again - and Paul's arm slid around her waist.

Then at last Stephen asked, 'Do you hear them?'

'Hear what?' Paul replied with a frown on his face.

'The bees!'

Paul looked at Joan with a concerned look on his face. The bees were making the usual noise they did when they visited - they were buzzing.

Stephen turned and looked at them. He appeared to gleam in the sunlight. 'I asked if you heard them.'

There was a brief pause before Paul asked, 'The bees?'

The two of them stood quietly and eventually Stephen nodded. He was forty-nine years old and had a face that was as wrinkled as leather and eyes that were as grey as the sea.

Then Joan spoke. 'Yes, they're nice,' she said.

'Nice?' Stephen turned away, staring at the hundreds of bees that were humming around the beehives, then after a moment he turned back and came walking over to them. There was an awkward silence as he just stared at them, saying nothing. It was at that moment that Paul knew his uncle had lost it. He had finally lost his marbles; he had lost his battle with senile dementia. However, he was surprised that he had lost it so soon. At forty-nine years old.

'It's a lovely afternoon,' Joan tried to change the subject.

'It would be if it weren't for them,' said Stephen.

'The bees, you used to love them!' Joan said.

Stephen seemed to go rigid. His gaunt throat moved. Then he said, 'Let's go into the house and have a cup of coffee.'

Once inside the confines of the kitchen it was so gloomy Stephen had to switch on the light. It cast up formless shadows of them on the walls.

When the coffee was ready Joan sipped and relished the taste of the hot liquid as it trickled its way down her throat, making her shiver.

'So what about the bees?' asked Paul.

Stephen sighed and put his mug down. 'I don't know whether I should tell you,' he said. He eyed them carefully. Joan felt restless under his gaze and reached out to take another sip of her drink.

Stephen dug into the pocket of his shirt and pulled out a notebook.

'There,' he said.

'What is it?' Paul asked.

'It's a code book,' said Stephen.

They watched him pour more coffee into his mug before he finally spoke again. 'It's the code of the bees,' he said.

Joan shuddered. She didn't know why. There was nothing terrible about the words. It was the way Stephen had spoken them. Stephen leaned forward, his eyes glowing in the weak light of the room.

'Listen,' he said, 'they aren't just making indiscriminate noises when they rapidly beat their wings together,' he paused. 'They're sending messages!' he said.

'Are you sure?' Paul asked.

'I'm sure,' said Stephen. He leaned in close. 'Have you ever really listened to bees? I mean really? If you had you'd have heard a rhythm to their noises. A pace, a definite beat. Well let me tell you something, since I started bee keeping I've listened and the more I listen the more I become convinced that their humming is a code. About a month after I started I suddenly heard a pattern. It's like a Morse Code only, of course, the sounds are different.'

Stephen stopped talking and looked at the black notebook.

'And there it is,' he said. 'I suddenly started deciphering it and here it is!' His throat worked convulsively as he picked his mug and finished off the rest of his drink.

'Well - what are they saying?' Paul asked awkwardly.

Stephen looked at him.

'Names,' his uncle told him. 'Look, I'll show you.'

He reached into one of his pockets and drew out a stubby pencil. Tearing a blank page from his notebook he started to write on it, muttering, to himself.

Paul and Joan looked at each other, knowing what each other was thinking without even having to tell each other - Paul's uncle was going to be going into the institution very soon.

Then they were looking into the garden and listening to the steady humming of the bees. Paul could see how that constant noise could drive a man to insanity. He suddenly felt guilty, and felt sad.

Stephen eventually put down the pencil. 'This will give you some idea,' he said, holding out the sheet for them to look at. Joan took it.

Lorna Coldman, it read. *James Kirby - David Pullman -*

'You see,' said Stephen, 'names.'

'Whose?' Joan had to ask even though she didn't want to.

Stephen held the book in a clenching hand.

'They are the names of the dead!' he answered.

Later that night, Joan climbed into bed with Paul and huddled close to him. 'I'm cold,' she murmured.

'You're scared.'

'Aren't you?'

'Well,' he said, 'I am but it isn't because of bees. I don't believe what he said, it's because I think he's finally lost his marbles.'

'Where'd he get those names?'

'Where anyone else would who was round the bend. Maybe they're friends of his,' he said. 'Maybe he made them up, maybe they're from tombstones.'

'Do you think he knows what we think?'

'I honestly don't know,' he said.

She snuggled against him. 'I'm glad you told him we were tired,' she said. 'I couldn't have taken much more,' she said.

They lay close to each other and slept. And, outside in the darkness, bees hummed, rapidly beating their wings together until morning came.

Stephen called at their house a week later. When they answered the door he barged in and said, 'You've got to help me.'

Paul's mouth tightened. 'Help you how?' he asked.

'Last night they kept on saying my name!'

'Who, the bees?' Joan asked, jadedly.

'Uncle,' Paul was trying to sound patient.

'Understand me,' Stephen pleaded. 'I know you think I'm crazy, but the bees are the ones who collect the dead! People think it's Death or the Grim Reaper or whatever name they give him but it's them! The bees! Every name they say the person dies just after.'

Stephen threw the local newspaper into Paul's lap. It was open at the obituary section. Three names were circled; all had died within the last week. The names were Lorna Coleman, James Kirby and David Pullman.

Lorna Coleman and David Pullman had died of cardiac arrests whilst James Kirby had died after a six year battle with cancer.

'This doesn't prove anything!' Paul argued.

Stephen's hands trembled. 'You're too ignorant to realise!' His throat moved convulsively. 'They'll come whether you decide to help me or not!' he said.

After a moment, Paul asked, 'What makes you so certain about this?'

'As I told you I've been writing this down ever since I deciphered their code and every name they speak the person dies shortly after. This has been going on all the time,' said Stephen, 'please believe me. I'm not crazy, they spelled out my name.'

Paul broke the heavy silence.

'What can we do?' he asked in a voice that bordered on uneasiness.

'Let me stay here with you,' said Stephen, 'so they can't get me.'

Joan looked nervously at Paul.

She is beginning to believe his crazy story, Paul thought to himself.

'I won't bother you,' said Stephen, 'I won't even sit here; I'll sit across the room. Just so, I can see you.'

That night they sat and watched television for most of the evening, but when Stephen went to the bathroom Joan asked Paul. 'What do we do now?'

'We'll have to let him stay until he gets this crazy idea out of his head.'

'How long will that be?'

'Honey, who knows what's going on in that head of his? I don't want to take any chances.'

Joan closed her eyes and exhaled wearily. 'What a way to spend a Saturday evening.'

Paul was about to speak again when he became conscious of the humming sound from outside. He got off of the sofa and looked out of the kitchen window. In the garden were hundreds of bees.

Joan was standing next to him. 'Do you think there's anything to this?'

'Let's hope not.' For the first time since she had known him there was a tremor in Paul's voice.

He tried to listen to the bees' noise and find some point of comparison with what his uncle had written in that notebook of his. He couldn't.

Then Stephen entered the room. 'They've come here for me.'

'It's just a coincidence.' Paul tried to reassure him.

The old man smiled. 'You know that's rubbish as well as I do.'

'Would it make you feel better if we all slept down here in the living room tonight?' Joan asked Stephen.

'I think it would,' he told them.

'I'll get the duvets,' Paul said and went upstairs.

'I'll make us all some cocoa.' Joan smiled and padded into the kitchen.

'That would be nice.' Stephen sat at the kitchen table as Joan made the drinks and stared out of the kitchen window at the swarm of bees that were now gathering outside in their hundreds.

It was after four in the morning when the screaming woke them. Paul felt Joan's fingers clutching at his arm as they both jolted to a sitting position, staring into the darkness. It was stone cold in the living room and their breath fogged before them in the gloom.

'What is it?' gasped Joan.

'I don't know.' Paul threw off the covers and dropped his feet to the floor.

The living room had a dim bulb burning overhead. Paul sprinted over the carpet towards the armchair where Stephen was sleeping. As soon as he reached his uncle a scream gagged inside his throat.

Lying in a pool of blood-splotched moonlight was Stephen, his skin swollen and raked open as if by a thousand tiny razor blades. The living room window was open - that was why the room was so cold. Joan stood paralysed, a fist pressed against her mouth while Paul moved to his uncle's side. He knelt down beside the motionless man and felt at Stephen's chest where the pyjama top had been sliced to ribbons. The faintest of heartbeats pulsed beneath his trembling fingers.

Stephen opened his eyes. Wide, staring eyes that recognised nothing, that looked right through Paul.

'P.a.u.l W.i.l.l.i.a.m.s.o.n.' Stephen spelled out the name in a bubbling voice. 'J.o.a.n P.l.e.a.s.a.n.c.e,' spelled Stephen, eyes stark and glazed.

His chest lurched once. Then his eyes began focusing on Paul. There was a terrible rattling in his throat as though the sounds were wrenched from in one by one by a power beyond his own.

Then they were alone with a dead man. And outside in the garden, hundreds of bees rapidly beat their wings together. And waited.

THE BLACK AND WHITE PHOTOGRAPH
Emma Lockyer

One lazy hot afternoon, I drove to my grandad's farm, way out in the sticks. He had died quite suddenly, and now I was on my way to his farm to collect some things before the movers come, and sell the rest for auction. I am going to sell the old place, and I shall miss it. It was the place I grew up, but I am not a farmer, and I have no brothers and sisters to help me or take over. So for the last time, I turn up the dirt road that leads to my grandad's place. There it stands like an old friend, same as always, welcoming and smiling, happy to see me. I feel a pinch of sadness; perhaps because I am missing the old man, and the old lady, she died last fall. I still remember the cookies that she used to bake before I arrived, knowing that the smell would have me running up to her in expectation.

It seemed all strange to me now, there were no familiar smells, no welcoming sounds, just the car making its way up to the house. I turned off the engine, and got out, yes everything was just as I remembered it. The swings down by the pond, the old tractor, that I used to use as a castle when I was little, that old tractor gave out years ago, yet still it stood. The water tower, with the weather vane on top of it, turning in the early afternoon breeze, yes everything was just the same.

I made my way up the small flight of stairs up to the front door, the door panels were faded now, but they were still showing the same colour green. Inside the air was kind of old and musty, Grandad had not been able to keep the old place going since Grandma died, but he had insisted on not going anywhere else, this was home and these were his things. I felt another pang of sadness, how could I get rid of all of his things? They were the only things left, to remind me of both of them. All of their things would become someone else's property, or thrown away. I had my own house filled with someone's else's treasures, mostly bought on flea markets, or antique stores, they sure don't build things like they used to anymore. Old things seem to have more value, more memories, and they sure do last a long time. I walked into the sitting room; it was large and comfortable, with the long six-seater sofa, the three-seater sofa, and the two single chairs by the fire. The fireplace was just as huge as the sofa, Grandad had built it himself, when he remodelled the house, just after my mother was born. He built four extra bedrooms and my grandmother filled them all with children. I could only imagine how happy those times were, all of the children on Christmas Day making a loud noise coming down the stairs.

I walked over to the mantelpiece, and still there were the black and white photographs my grandmother had put in silver frames, of my mother and my three uncles. My uncles had gone on to do other things, none of them had wanted to stay on at the farm and help their dad. Uncle Rodger was now a dentist with his own practice, Denver was a businessman, making and selling blinds for conservatories, uncle Bill had become a captain on a cruiseliner. My mother had become a housewife, with no such interest in farming, but she did become a florist, and has her own chain of shops. I remember that she once had a keen passion for taking photographs, and was forever taking photographs of me. I could see a couple of examples of her work, both of them in colour, but the ones I remember fondly were the ones in black and white, they were all of my uncles, and Grandad and Grandma, just as I recall them happy and smiling.

I lifted a frame with a picture of my mother sitting on the swing outside, and dropped a photograph onto the floor. I picked it up and straight away noticed that it was of me, a black and white photograph of myself stood in front of the barn, Grandad's old barn. I had forgotten all about the old photo, I was wearing a pink and white dress, my blonde hair was in plaits, and I was wearing short white socks, with the shoes I wore for school. I was happy because Grandma was making Sunday lunch, and we were going to have it outside.

The old barn was still standing when I arrived, but looking at in the picture, it looked newer and fresher. There was a sign on the outside saying, *no smoking in barn;* I guess Grandad had to remind himself! The sign is still there, faded but recognisable. I looked very small compared to the barn; the opening above my head was huge and black. I could not quite make out what was behind me in the barn, but I knew Grandad kept his tractor in there, and all of the other heavy equipment that he used around the farm. Either side of the barn were some bushes and young trees, I remember that Grandad had planted them himself outside the barn, I think he was not too keen on the barn sticking out like a sore thumb, and the trees would cover most of it eventually. I think he was right, you just don't see the barn anymore, you see the trees first, and you really don't notice the barn at all. Good old grandad, he sure knew a thing or two about trees, he could tell you all of their names and what they were good for. The mantelpiece was made from green oak.

'It will last for hundreds of years', I could just imagine him saying, after he had built the fireplace. I gave a heavy sigh, 'I sure miss you Grandad, and this is the hardest day of my life trying to say goodbye. Goodbye to you, your house, and your farm.' A surge of tears filled my eyes, and I wiped them away with a sniff, such sentimentality was not going to get the job done. I was here for a reason, my mother had asked me to meet her here, and she still had not arrived. I made a point to phone her from my cell phone, in a few more minutes, just enough time to get over the sadness I was now feeling.

It was then that I noticed the dust in the picture, maybe the lens was not clean enough to take the picture properly, no, it was some dandelion fluff or seeds of something else. I needed to get Grandad's old magnifying glass out from the drawer next to his chair. He always used it to read the papers, never bothering to buy glasses. *'If I needed them all of the time I would bother buying some'*, he would say. With the magnifying glass in my hand, I could see more clearly now, yes dandelion fluff next to my face, and above my head . . . I could not believe it! . . . A small body of a fairy . . . with wings, in the air . . . her arms outstretched like she was dancing on the breeze! But I had never seen this before ! . . . Why now? How? My mind became a myriad of questions. Who took the photograph? Now I remember it was Grandad! He had said something that came back to me on that day; that the farm had its own magic, and it was a special place. He had felt it when he first arrived, and had had always felt the magic of the place, even when he was away. I had not paid much attention at the time, but his words were being heard loud and clear now, this was a magic place!

I picked up the cell phone and dialled my mother.

'Mother, I thought you were supposed to meet me here; it's gone two thirty!'

'Meet you where honey? I have been in the shop all afternoon, I never asked to meet you anywhere today.'

'But you phoned me this morning and said you would be here at 1pm!'

'No I did not honey, I never made such a phone call, I have been too busy working all day, I have a wedding order to finish by tomorrow at the latest, I have not got the time to come and meet you.'

'But who was that on the phone?'

'I don't know honey, must have been one of your friends.'

I could not believe that she would just lie to me like that, why would she lie? Was she lying?

I looked up at the mantelpiece, and at all of the familiar people smiling at me, they somehow held the answer. Whatever the mystery was they were keeping it, all I was going to get was their smiles. There on the end of the mantelpiece was another photograph of Grandad reading the newspaper; I had never seen this picture before, must have been taken by my mum, or grandmother. It was just how I remembered him, deep in thought, studying the print. He was holding it out so you could just make out the headlines, if I used the magnifying glass again, I could get an idea of when it was taken. There, under the headline local news:-

Seth Granger's grandaugher Bernice, has decided to turn her grandfather's old farm into a teashop, come garden centre, using the skills her mother has acquired creating a chain of flower shops across the state. Bernice said she could not get rid of the old place, and it would have broken her grandfather's heart, if he was still alive, to see the old place go. The old Granger farm has now become famous since a black and white photograph, featuring Bernice as a child, was discovered to have a fairy dancing above Bernice's head.

LONG TAIL
Ian W Robinson

Scuttle, scuttle-sniff - whiskers twitch, paws scamper, a sinuous tail curves around a candlestick, abandoned on its side, at the foot of the altar steps.

Stopping! The long tail scented the darkening pool, took a tentative lick, then an enthusiastic slurp - *free food*, from a glutinous morass seeping from beneath the door of the confessional box.

To identify the dusty corpse inside the confessional, lay only a white collar, denoting a priest . . . ?

A child's footsteps clattered over the stone flags, oaken portals slammed shut. The cold breeze chuckled as it crept beneath the slowly opening door of the confessional, down the aisle, followed by twirling, snaking shadows, rippling over the brown fur, enveloping the long tail, leaving a husk - bones which crumbled to dust. The breeze moaning, sighing, chuckling to itself, moved amongst the granite columns, causing the insidious mist, to swirl back through the Nave, shrouding the sacred altar and smothering the gold cross of Christ.

The once proud tower clock whimpered twelve o'clock on the eve of Hallowe'en.

The old lady staggered under the weight of autumn blooms she brought to decorate the cathedral. She laid the flowers on the steps while she hunted through her handbag for her keys.

Finding them she selected one and inserted it into the lock, surprisingly the door swung silently, especially as it should have been locked; it seemed that the hinges had been recently greased.

Picking up the flowers, she cautiously entered the hallowed Nave, her footsteps echoed hollowly in the silence of the building. Looking up, she gasped in horror, the sacred altar and cross had been burnt. Turning, she ran in front of the pews, towards the confessional box, slamming into the half opened door. Spinning, she collapsed on the floor, her knees sinking into the red morass, handing kneading the flour like dust. Her eyes opened wide in terror as she saw the white collar. Her mouth opened, a high pitched whine, reaching a screaming crescendo, emitted from the red lipped cavern. Regaining her feet, she flew from the building as fast as her arthritic feet would allow, grateful for the safety of the sunlight.

The building bathed in the early morning light, looked exactly what it was - a 'Police Station'. Moss covered the roof, one or two ridge tiles missing; the occupants weren't concerned with the water running down the walls, it was only in a little used cell. The brickwork was shabby, paintwork peeling. All in all, matching the rather run down and seedy looking market town, nestling under the spectre of the cathedral.

Visitors to the establishment would be forgiven for thinking that the building was not in fact a police station but an establishment for the homeless, drug addicts, alcoholics and general down and outs.

The constable behind the counter was bored. With his tired looking uniform, he half-heartedly completed entries in the charge book. The book itself looked as tired and dilapidated as its surroundings, with its curled yellowing pages, coffee and ink stains marking the weeks, months, years' entries.

To the right of the counter; stood a partly opened door; with the stencilled legend CID; from where an indistinct murmur emanated.

Suddenly the telephone sounded a discordant note. A scrimmage occurred amongst the pile of old papers, half-filled coffee cups and discarded cigarette ends. Eventually a finely manicured hand lifted the receiver.

A tall slender man, in a hand-stitched suit spoke into the mouthpiece.

'Hello, yes it's - DI Germaine speaking?'

He listened intently to the caller.

'Mmm, mmm, who's speaking? - Hello, damn it!'

Angry silence prevailed while he searched for a piece of paper. Finding some, he impatiently scribbled down the information, in the process, knocking over an overflowing ashtray, its contents joining their companions on the floor.

Handing the piece of paper to the other occupant of the room, he issued instructions. 'Right Sergeant, be off with you, and take one of the plods to St Ninians,' he shouted. 'It's now nine-thirty, make sure you get back to me before one o'clock and be quick about it!'

'Yes Inspector,' replied the sergeant, closing the door behind him.

Fenris, stirred in the chair, rubbing his eyes and running his fingers through his tousled hair. His cat was sitting, remonstrating with him about not going to bed and not waking up at the normal time, so that she and her companion could be fed and exercised together.

Yes, alright. But I had to study. I've got to find a chink in his armour - human or supernatural; they all make a mistake sooner or later. OK I'm getting up. Placing his hand on the chair arm to lever himself up, a warm tongue washed it.

Drawing the curtains he saw that it was a crisp autumn day.

He suddenly shuddered; he knew his adversary would be on the move again today. Completing his morning ritual, he drained the last of the coffee before donning his jacket and calling the dog. Opening the door, he suddenly felt a thud on his shoulders and a loud purring in his ear. He turned his head slightly and looked at the cat. *So you want to come this morning eh?* The purring continued and the black and white face rubbed itself against his cheek. *OK let's go then.*

He arrived back at the flat, just as the telephone shrilled. Closing the front door and struggling to remove his jacket, he picked up the handset.

'Yes? Yes Fenris speaking. Who is this? - Damn it!' he swore, as he replaced the receiver.

Picking up his jacket, making sure he had his keys, and calling the dog to 'Stay - Guard,' he closed the door and dashed to his car.

Damn it, I should have known something was going to happen, but I didn't reckon so soon.

He was about to turn right at the lights, when an ambulance swung in front of him and pulled up at the cathedral steps, with its lights flashing. Police cars, blue lights, competing with pirouetting flash bulbs of the press, danced in a cacophony of light. *Damn it!* Fenris swore to himself.

The vicious *brrring*, brought the Inspector out of his reverie, he dived for the phone spilling papers left and right.

'Hello - yes Sergeant? Tell me man, what happened - is the old biddy sure? Yes - right, I'll be over shortly, just concentrate, make sure the crime scene's clear OK?'

The inspector wondered why churches and religion always haunted him? He'd had enough in France with the bloody bishops - narrow minded fools. Shrugging his shoulders, he thought he'd put all that and the sodding kids, behind him.

Arriving at the cathedral, he threw open the car door.

'Get them bloody spectators back - now Sergeant!' he bawled at the flustered figure.

'I'm trying to sir, but they're getting ugly - sir,' the sergeant replied.

Germaine opened the oak doors, he faintly smelled the odour of sulphur, he shuddered.

Turning from the open doorway he shouted at the sergeant, 'Sergeant, keep that crowd back - now get four men in here and where's the ambulance?'

'It's coming sir,' replied the hapless man.

The Inspector turned and waited for them to carry out his orders.

Hearing the footsteps behind him, he looked back and coldly asked, 'Where are the other two men?'

'I've only got two men sir, the rest are on other duties.'

Sighing, he beckoned the men to follow him.

'Keep your hands in your pocket - fool - I said don't touch anything until forensics get here - *I suppose you did send for them?*' He addressed the last comment to the luckless sergeant.

'Yes sir - they shouldn't be too long.'

The Inspector shuddered at the sight of the grunge and dust at the confessional. Looking at the scorched altar, he gave a hardly perceptive sign, but he had been badly shaken at the sight of the cross and altar showing so much damage.

'Look, the altar has been moved - come on you men!'

As the men came closer, the Inspector shouted at them. *'Stop now! You there!'* pointing to a constable, 'get another pair of hands immediately!'

The man ran off to obey. He came back shortly with a wizened hunchback of a man.

'I said a man not a dwarf - I suppose he'll do,' he said sarcastically to the officer.

'He's the gardener sir and he's reputed to be very strong,' replied the constable.

'We'll see,' was the reply.

'Now get behind the altar and move it this way - there is a pit of some sort beneath it, don't fall in,' the Inspector commanded.

'Look - there's a green light - God, the smell's lousy,' one of the men announced.

Suddenly there was a sound of rustling and squealing - then an eruption of furry bodies with glowing red eyes swarmed over the lip of the pit.

A piercing scream cleft the air, a second followed, as the tidal wave of rats covered two of the unfortunate police officers - eating them alive.

Struck dumb, the Inspector could only look on in horror, turning he noticed a black shadow swirling around the pillars in the Nave. 'God save me,' he begged.

'Nothing can save you. Your bishop's cursed you; your God doesn't want you after the things your did to those children,' the voice boomed out of the swirling shadow. Germaine whirled round trying to see where the voice had come from, his eyes widened as he saw the shadow shroud his sergeant and the hunchback.

A scream echoed around the cathedral. As the shadow moved away from where the two figures had stood, he noticed the throbbing, dusty remains, of the dwarf. He trembled as he saw the figure of his sergeant metamorphosing into a rearing black charger with slashing hooves, glistening fangs, flames billowing from its nostrils and glowing red-hot coals for eyes.

The shadow surrounded Germaine. As it crushed his whole being into dust, his screams echoed around the ancient walls.

'You're mine!' the cold voice dripping with venom, spat the words out with a gush of foul fumes. *'Mine.'* The words of the *Collector of Souls,* hung in the fetid air, as the wave of longtails flowed back to the pit.

Suddenly the large bells started to toll, only one person could hear them, as he arrived at the cathedral steps.

Fenris pushed through the crowds, looking for a familiar face. Suddenly a hand roughly grabbed him, spinning him around. 'Christ, it's you!' Fenris said as he recognised the scruffy reporter. 'You phoned me?'

'Yes,' the weasel-faced man replied. 'Shut up and listen for a moment! The police are keeping shtum, they look scared. Six are dead including Inspector Germaine and a priest.' The reporter's voice tailed off.

'Can you get me in; it's very important?' Fenris pleaded.

'Yes, I've got a spare press badge - but I want the exclusive - deal?'

'Yes - yes. Just give me the badge and stay here!' Fenris held out his hand. *I don't think this will be one exclusive you're likely to want,* Fenris muttered.

After viewing the carnage in the cathedral, Fenris was glad to be in fresh air and daylight. He spotted the reporter trying to blend in with the stonework. Fenris grabbed his arm, 'Christian, come with me!'

Both marched to the nearest cafe. Sitting down at a table a girl brought him a cup of coffee.

'Where's mine?' Christian whined.

Fenris spat out, 'You disobeyed me.'

Christian started to speak.

Fenris interrupted. 'You sneaked in. You were standing behind the altar,' he barked. 'You've paid the price. You were stupid, you preyed on the innocent.'

A cold look shut Christian up.

'You're dead - the Collector of Souls - he's coming for you!' Fenris hissed.

Christian wept as Fenris left.

AN ARTISTIC SOLUTION
Kathleen Townsley

Lisa was hurrying home from work in the rush hour, she smiled to herself and turned her head to glance behind her, she saw the same young man exactly three feet behind, never gaining and never decreasing the space between them, she continued on her way, determined not to turn round again, that was her big mistake, and one of the reasons her life ended a few minutes later. The man knew she was watching him but carried on keeping the same pace, after all his best killings always started the same way, pick your victim and keep behind at exactly the same pace, never veering off course. He knew she would stop looking, and become complacent, that is what he relied on, he kept the same distance, even when she stepped to the edge of the kerb, and waited with the rest of the people for the lights to change at the crossing, he knew how long she had to wait, and just as they were about to change he closed in. Pulling the knife out of his pocket he lunged, perfect again, as her legs buckled the lights changed and the people surged forward, he turned and walked away, homeward to relive the excitement. He had never been good with the opposite sex, yet this way they all wanted to know who he was, they all thought they knew why he followed them, wondering if he would ask them out on a date, he knew he was a good looking man, his mother was always telling him and his mother was always right, once again the headlines in the paper tomorrow would read, 'Victim number five for the crossing killer'. His mother would be so proud; one day he would tell her of his success and then he would see the praise in her eyes for her clever son, the praise he had always longed for, and the praise he now deserved.

Chief Inspector Lowry was furious as he stepped into the station, how many weeks had this been going on? What on earth was CID doing? He had given them extra men, agreed overtime and still no convictions. The phone rang and Inspector Stubbs lifted the receiver. 'CID Inspector Stubbs,' he said.

'I suggest you hide,' said his friend and colleague Sergeant Painter. 'I've just seen Lowry heading in your direction and he is not a happy chap.'

'Thanks,' said Stubbs, 'when is he ever?' and replaced the receiver. Just then the door burst open and in walked Lowry, Stubbs rose from his seat just enough so the air could circulate, then sat down again.

'What the hell is going in here?' Lowry shouted, 'I have given you all you requested and received nothing in return.'

Stubbs sat and waited for the torrent to finish, he knew Lowry would have to stop for breath sometimes, when he did, he took great pleasure in telling him that at last they had a breakthrough, the lady who had been killed was very chatty and had told everyone at work that the same man had followed her every night for a whole week, and she was hoping that last night would be the night he made his move to ask her out.

'He did that alright,' said Lowry, 'but not the invitation she was expecting, and how does that help? Unless she assembled all her fellow workers together and they all went back to her flat for tea, thus enabling them to see this man, we are again where we started, and that is exactly nowhere, it's not as if we do not have a connection, all the victims lived, in those flats, surely someone saw something.'

Stubbs swallowed and said, 'I was down at the flats again this morning and all the residents have been re-interviewed, no one knows anything. The young man in the ground floor flat was helpful as usual, he must be sick of us appearing on his doorstep, yet he has the full view of the main entrance and can therefore see all who enter or leave the flats, never going out much due to his mother, he always welcomes us, but then being such a nice patient man, of which, if I might say, is a rarity these days.' As he said this he looked straight at Lowry, 'No new evidence has come to light, we are now interviewing everyone at the young lady's workplace.'

Chief Inspector Lowry glared at Stubbs and said, 'So what you are saying is, even with all the extra police officers, you still are none the wiser,' then standing up as he left the office allowing the door to slam behind him.

Stubbs picked up the phone and asked for his car to be brought round, he would visit the flats again, maybe he would get lucky. The young man was pleased to see Inspector Stubbs, for as he said, being housebound for most of the day except when the nurse arrived to see to his mother, allowing him to go to the shops, he rarely had company. *A lovely man,* thought Stubbs, even with his slightly bent gait, and deformed left hand, which he had never tried to conceal, the answers remained the same. Thanking him for his kindness he left him to go about his business, for he had enough to do without Stubbs getting under his feet. Yet, something kept niggling at the back of his mind, and he decided to run through the CCTV footage again. Everyone near the crossing had been interviewed, the only one unaccounted for was the figure leaving the scene as the lights changed, but this man had kept his back to the camera, and had even stooped a little so as not to be detected, therefore only a guess at the man's height could be made, even so something was familiar, but he could not bring this to mind. The man was again detected on the CCTV as he entered the underground station, but he had remained close to the wall, and they only had half of a back view of the man, again he had been bent slightly to hide his height, and though the jacket and trousers appeared the same nothing else could be seen. He had even kept his hand in his pocket, this they had all agreed was to conceal the knife he had just used in the attack. The phone rang, it was Turner, he had just spoken to a young lady who having just returned from her holidays that morning, and following a short sleep had called into work to collect her work roster for the following week, therefore had not been interviewed earlier that day, she was extremely upset, being a good friend of the victim's. When he told Stubbs what she had said, a smile lit up Stubbs face, he put a call through to Lowry. When the Inspector answered, Stubbs said, 'it appears this young lady was also a budding artist and has drawn the man, she gave it to her friend to see before her friend went on holiday. Turner has just gone to collect the drawing from the young lady's home, and then hopefully we will know her killer.'

Stubbs and Lowry were sat in Stubbs office having coffee, awaiting Turner's return, they both sat in silence, they had nothing in common, both police officers moved in different circles, the chief at his country club, whilst Stubbs preferred the local pub, he was still thinking about the CCTV footage when a thought flashed through his head, but again it eluded him, there was something he was definitely missing, frowning he tried to concentrate going over and over in his head the events of the day.

Turner arrived back and placed the picture on the table, it was unmistakable, the features as clear as day, jumping up he grabbed his coat and ran out of the office leaving Lowry sitting there with his mouth open. Turner followed close behind. Soon they were heading out of the yard and towards the flats; Stubbs sat quietly, and thought, *what a fool I have been, he certainly fooled me and the rest of the team, a kind and friendly man and a credit to his manhood, not many single blokes would take care of their mother, bedridden as she was,* a lot of people he knew would have put her in a home and thrown away the key. Well respected by everyone at the flats by all accounts, *how wrong can you be?* He must have interviewed him at least three if not four times since the murders began, even twice today he had spoken to him, not a hunch or twinge did he feel, the man certainly pulled the wool over my eyes but not anymore. That was the fifth murder in as many months, till today no clues at all, the same death every time, the lights change, people surge to get to the other side and everyone who crossed assumed the young lady had fallen, till one unlucky soul stopped to give her a hand, thus discovering the murder.

This time he would not get away, as the two cars turned into the estate and headed towards the flats, Stubbs and Turner both leapt out of the car as soon as it came to a halt, and ran all the way up to the main doors. After banging on door of flat number one, and announcing their arrival, it seemed an age before the door opened and the man in the sketch stood before them. The man stepped aside and let them in leaving two constables, whom they had collected on their dash from the station, outside the door.

'How can I help you gentlemen?' he said, 'you have just caught me, I was preparing to go to the shops when the nurse arrives, she is very punctual, always arrives at four-thirty, never varies, it allows me to catch the shops before they close, do come in, and please close the door behind you.' Then turning he walked down the hallway, it was then that Inspector Stubbs saw the light, as he followed the young man down the hallway it hit him right between the eyes, from the back the young man appeared to be bending and he noticed he had his left hand tucked in his coat pocket, the same coat that was visible from the CCTV footage. Still he tried to bluff his way through the reasons for the officers sudden visit, he continued to chatter away and only stopped when looking at the Inspector's face, his shoulders seemed to slump even lower and he stopped talking long enough to be read his rights and arrested for the murder of the five young women.

'How did you know? I was so careful, never veered off the chosen path, I was certain you would never catch me. I have always been very particular in anything I do, my mum says it is one of my better faults.'

'Simple,' said Stubbs as they escorted him to the waiting car, 'you chose the wrong girl this time, a clever girl, loved drawing when at school, one of her favourite subjects, had you down to a fine art she did. Never really been interested in paintings myself,' said Stubbs, 'could never understand it, but I will now look at art in a different light, maybe I'll take it up,' then looking at the man he said, 'then again I am a busy man but you will have a lot of time on your hands.'

'I was never good with writing implements,' said the man. 'Mother always saw to things like that.'

Then as the man was placed into the back seat of the car Inspector Stubbs said, 'Shame about that, we all need to draw a line sometime in our lives.'

THE VISITATION
Peter Jennison

In the cold and damp of a January day, with the fields and lanes looking hoary in the mist, and trees that shiver in the overcast sky, quite naked, I set off to visit the old house. Just why I should choose such a day for my visit I do not know. But here I am in the twilight hour, alone with my thoughts and that eerie silence which comes to desolate places at nightfall. Just above my head is a huge dead elm, whose towering limbs support rambling knots of ivy. The hedge is overgrown, and the two stone gateposts standing in the night remind me instantly of tombstones. I tread in the gravel and the sound leaps up, a stray wild brier scrapes my sleeve, and all along the path, the shadowy shrubs and the deeper pockets of darkness. As I pass between the posts, I see the once bright borders barren and heaped with last year's leaves. Then the crumbling old house, black against the sky, just a vague, grey shape in the misty dusk, crouching forlorn and abandoned. And everywhere so still and silent round the house, yet I feel a thousand eyes are watching. But then perhaps there are? - I see the bats are out.

I enter the porch and disturb something sleeping in the rafters. A flutter in panic, now the scurrying away, now the silence. I step back a yard to let the creature escape and feel the damp wings in my face. Then a look round swiftly sees nothing of the bird, just trees in the dusk and the half dozen cottages empty and abandoned further on. These buildings on the cliffs which have fallen to the sea are full of ghosts. I open the door and the room stares back, I fumble in my pocket for a match. In the mirror on the wall I see the pale round moon reflected.

Should I go on with this or turn away? At this moment, on the step, my feelings are inclined towards latter. But an end must be made for my own peace of mind, though I don't know just why I am here. I strike another match and look inside, nothing! By the hearth are some logs, and a few thin sticks lay scattered loosely in the grate. I decide to go in and light a fire.

The room feels damp and smells musty, cobwebs keep catching in my hair, the clock on the wall has stopped at something past eleven. But apart from these, everything is just as I remember it. There is the bureau in the corner, the sideboard down the wall, Helena's old chair by the hearth. As I move further in, I feel a presence of some sort, as if death has touched the house and a spirit haunts the pale glow of moonlight. I light the sticks and they begin to splutter, the old oak beams give a crack; was that an owl outside?

Suddenly I start and look sharply at the door. Some footsteps are coming down the path. I hold myself stiff and wait for the knock, but no knock is ever delivered. Then a voice calls out from as close as the porch but through the porch window I see no one. I move towards the door and open it, and see only what looks like a white collar floating unsupported in the pitch black beneath the trees. My heart skips a beat as I remember the voice and that its owner, the vicar, is dead. Then I see the thing slowly coming out of the trees, slowly, slowly towards the cliffs, a distance now from the back of the house of less than twenty-five strides. I follow in pursuit though I know not why, wondering at myself and the strange unexplainable phenomena. Yet there's nothing from the tops but the noise of the sea and the pale glimmer of moonlight.

And the monochrome beach is of another world. The sea, a huge black void with white edges foaming and hissing at the night. And the moon, a full, round globe of white light hard and solitary, sprinkling a trail of frosty sparks upon the water. But the wispy clouds, they could easily be ghosts, casting their shadows across the dark cliffs, seeking, peering in the hollows. Then the roar of the sea and the vast black sky, the moon, the clouds, the isolation, and all across the tops the sound of the wind moaning softly as in grieving, touching the night with a wearied woe, calling to the many dead souls. I turn from the cliffs and hurry back to the house.

'A large slug of whisky,' I say to myself as I shoot the bolt on the door. I had brought a flask of the finest malt and some sandwiches. After this, I sit quietly in Helena's old chair and stare vacantly at the fire. A warm scent is rising from the burning logs, a scent made damp by the fusion of steam from the ones on the hearth put to dry. Soon I feel drowsy and slip into idle reminiscence. How well I remember the terrible gale of that fateful night last November. I stare at the brightness leaping in the grate and feel the flickering shadows on the walls. A large black spider crawls from the hearth and scurries away across the rug. Then all is still on this winter's night, with only the sound of distant waves, the flickering of firelight and me. If Helena intends to visit me tonight I will be here for her.

But morning arrives as mornings sometimes do, with mist on the breath and that clammy touch to the fingers. The dawn feels icy and stillborn, the room damp, sepulchral. The fire is out and the grey ash has settled in the gate, and that strange uneasiness which comes with this hour is on me. Perhaps a tiny glimmer, not yet light but not pure dark, is at the window. I pull my coat more tightly round my shoulders. Suddenly I see her in the pattern on the wall, there! - between the curtain and the door. Then I see her again, more distinctly this time, her form emerging slowly from the faint shadows on the wall. In a shroud of silk, and with golden hair, her pale face shining in the darkness. But is it really the Helena I love?

In the panic of the moment I sit open-mouthed and simply stare at her. She is little more yet than a plume of vapour against the wall. Minute particles, little more than dust, begin to group together and intensify. Then a bright spot in the centre turns a shade of pink and starts to pulse regularly like a heart. No sound is uttered and the silence runs on, though I fancy her pale lips to move. Then she flits across the room with the ease of a cloud, passing through a chair and the dining table and out through the bolted door.

I sit transfixed, wide-eyed, open-mouthed, watching her. She was half expected yet when, in the end, she had actually appeared I am terrified. The dawn is not yet and all is still, but excited and alarmed I flee outside to the morning. In the pale eerie light the trees look overbearing and menacing, the overgrown shrubs about to pounce, and the tangled hedge, treacherous and alive with spiders. Through the limbs of the elm I see her pass through the branches and on, silently towards the church. And the church is a ruin and derelict now, only the bats live there. I follow on behind, going after her.

You see Helena, my sister was swept away. The storm of that night took the back of the house and swept her away to the sea. The vicar was swept away also, and much in love were the vicar and my sister and their bodies have never been found. If only I knew they had gone together and were destined together for eternity.

I creep towards the gate then down the narrow path to the church. Everywhere looks derelict and abandoned. The rows of odd headstones at this hour and in this light are stark and frightening. They remind me of soldiers scattered by defeat, leaning, resting, shocked into terrible stillness. But the vicar and Helena are together on the path, each with their arms about the other! How wonderful to see they are still together and in love. Just a moment, no longer, and now they are gone, so that only the dawn and the rows of leaning gravestones remain. Then the gravestones fade also, they merge with the dawn, and I find myself again in Helena's chair.

I blink at the hearth, at the black uneven bars, at the white ash lying in the grate. The day is quite light and a low winter sun shines vaguely pink through the mist. I glance at the window then slowly round the room, not sure which cognition is reality. Then I hear a voice calling from the taxi in the lane and I spring to put my things together.

'Are you real?' I ask the driver as I hand him my bag. He sniffs, smiles, but never answers.

FEAR
Valerie E Pope

The cupboard was dark. In fact at first Ntashi was unable to see anything at all until her brown eyes had adapted to the blackness within the three foot confines of her small prison. Then she felt reassured by feeling around and finding several rolls of material, storage boxes and a pile of bibles. The nuns at the Catholic convent in the northern town of Ksali in the region of Birundi had placed Ntashi inside the wall cupboard as a punishment for giggling during prayers. She was often in trouble for she seemed to attract the naughtiest friends with her outgoing personality yet she was also often the child the strict nuns would single out for reprimand as if they could not abide to watch the little girl's sublime happiness and resilience in the aftermath of trauma. Ntashi had already experienced great tragedy in her short eight years of life. Both parents and her two sisters had been massacred in their village by the rebels and it was only because the child had been in the hospital recovering from measles that she had escaped the same fate . . .

The region of Rwanda where the convent was built, lay close to the border and was plagued by bands of rebels rampaging through the tiny scattered villages plundering and raping before setting fire to the brush and wooden homes. The nerves of the nuns were thus constantly on edge and this perhaps excused short tempers with the children in their charge and in particular for Ntashi's banishment to the cupboard for merely a small misdemeanour in the chapel.

The child philosophically decided to pass the time by singing hymns to herself as she was certain that one of the sisters, most probably Sister Benedict would come to let her out before the evening roll call and supper. She settled herself on a roll of material and hummed or sang her way through her repertoire of Christian songs before finally seeking the solace of her thumb (another sin, but then she thought to herself, *the nuns couldn't see her in here could they?*) Within a few minutes Ntashi was asleep.

In the convent, the sisters were gathered in the office of the Mother Superior listening to the disturbing news on the radio that the rebels were approaching their village. All persons were being advised to collect their belongings and run to the hills for cover. On hearing the warning the Mother Superior organised her sisters into teams, each responsible for a certain number of children and sent them to gather clothing and food as quickly as possible, ready for a swift departure into the forest. The younger nuns were frightened and looked to their leader for reassurance and spiritual guidance. She offered prayers for their deliverance and as soon as they had left the room, she desperately tried the telephone link to request assistance or protection but as she had suspected, the lines had already been cut by the rebels.

Fear gripped her stomach when she recalled the previous skirmishes she had experienced with drug crazed rebels. She felt physically sick as she considered what horror possibly lay before her sisters and their young charges, before the night was out.

At that moment a young man ran through the convent gates and flung himself at her feet begging for help. He was bleeding heavily from a huge gash across one shoulder and his body bore the deep marks of many other wounds from sharp knives and machetes. She helped him to sit up and lean against the wall as he told her in terror about the scene he had left behind at the neighbouring settlement church. The villagers there had been overrun early that morning and he believed everybody had been killed including the pastor, his wife and their three small children. He had witnessed villagers' hands hacked off, small babies snatched from their screaming frantic mothers, tossed into the air and murdered in front of their screaming parents.

The young men had been mutilated before being killed, then the older folk roughly herded into the forest and massacred in a frenzy of hate. The wretched young man wept desperately and again entreated for protection in the convent with the Mother Superior. She helped him to his feet and supported his body into the chapel where she gave him a carafe of water to drink, before assisting him to sit on a woven seat in the nave. She hastened outside to the courtyard just as the sisters and children carrying their bundles assembled at the central cross. The convent gardener who was in truth, merely a general handyman approached the sister and asked if he should toll the bell in the small chapel turret to summon assistance from their neighbours. He was unaware that the closest neighbouring villagers were probably already dead so the nun gently praised him for his suggestion and the man sped away to clang the bell for the glory of God and the hope of deliverance.

In the courtyard the voices of the exuberant young pupils rang through the air as their teachers tried to silence them by instilling the need to be quiet whilst they were fleeing into the forest. The serious faces of their teachers eventually hushed the children and they began to queue in orderly lines ready for instructions. Simultaneously the sound of men's shouting could be heard coming from outside the convent grounds. Immediately the Mother Superior ordered everybody in her care into the convent. 'Quiet now.' Gathering their small bundles in their skinny hands, obediently, the children hurried across the dusty yard and entered the cool chapel.

Behind them could now be heard the terrifying din of the perimeter fences being shaken in frenzy before the rendered noise of fractured palings as the boarding was smashed to the ground allowing access to the hoard of young wild men scrambling into the convent courtyard, brandishing axes, machetes, flailing long knives and waving sharpened wooden poles cut from trees on their approach through the forest.

The Mother Superior staunchly stood her ground as the rebel mob stormed around her, eyes staring, mouths wide open screaming obscenities, intoxicated with their power or alcohol and all of them overcome by a combined bloodlust . . . She bravely attempted to hide her terror by standing proudly to her full height, an imposing figure in the black and white habit, assuming a righteous anger and berating the leaders of the mob. When this seemed to have no response she began to plead for mercy and the lives of her sisters and their young charges. In answer a tall craze-eyed man leapt forward, arm raised, grasping a machete high in the air above his head. One violent action swathed the air leaving the nun's head lying bloodied in the dust of the courtyard, her white coif fluttering in the gust of hot air and her habit outstretched around her in the blood like a stricken bird . . . Watching this dreadful scene from the casement, the nuns in the chapel screamed in terror and attempted to pull shut the heavy wooden door but before they were able to fasten it against the rebel horde, it was forced back by the rampaging mob who swarmed and jostled its way into the cool holy place filled with terrified children. They began killing haphazardly, flailing the air with the weapons sending bloody splatters of blood over the freshly painted whitewashed walls and stone slabs on the floor. Within minutes the white stone walls were running with red, the polished wooden pews stood glistening with the body parts of little children and women, the plaster saints were overturned and lay among the horror. The figure of

Christ on His crucifix looked down on the massacre with pity in His soft eyes.

At the far end of the sanctuary stood an ancient mahogany piano, a relic from the old colonial era. As the murderous crowd surged through the chapel searching for any child or teacher left alive, a single blow from a machete landed on the yellowed ivory keys of the instrument producing a cacophony of discordant sound echoing the shrieking cries surrounding it. This seemed to enflame the revolutionaries, who then turned their wrath onto the inanimate piano and with a terrible mob insanity hacked it to a pile of splintered wood and jagged metal within minutes . . .

Suddenly the tumult ceased. It seemed as if this last senseless act of vandalism rather than the heinous child slaughter of a short while before, now acted as a catalyst on the butchering mob. The men lowered their weapons, viewed the indescribable carnage surrounding them and simply as a mass left the chapel moving on to the main convent building to search for church valuables, their collective blood lust sated for a while.

At the back of the chapel inside the cupboard, little Ntashi lay weeping silently. She had heard the screams through the walls and had instinctively realised the implication of the subsequent silence. Total fear overwhelmed her as she involuntarily soiled her underclothes. She felt blindly around on the wooden floor, down in the darkness and removed the white soiled pants frightened of the anger of the nuns, thankfully forgetting the probable fate of her schoolmates and teachers . . . Ntashi remained rigid on the roll of material for many hours, drifting off into a restless nightmarish sleep from time to time. As night fell she heard the key turned in the lock of the cupboard and felt a terrible horror curl through her tiny stomach clenching and squeezing it tight. She placed her clenched fists into her mouth to stifle the incipient screams but as the door slowly opened she could see the handyman standing in the doorway, peering into the gloom. Relief swept over the child. With a quiet childish dignity Ntashi slowly stood up, carefully picked up her damp knickers and placed her little hand in his large comforting grasp.

MURDER, SUICIDE, OR?
Ron Bird

Hazel never knew when the idea to kill her husband first came to her, it seemed to be in her head when they came back from their honeymoon, when she had found out what a mean, selfish, chauvinist pig of a man he really was. Not at all the charming man he had pretended to be during their whirlwind seven month courtship, when he had treated her like a lady and spent money on her like it was going out of fashion. They had met when she had taken a job as barmaid at a lovely old country club, it was to be only temporary while she was resting between acting work. Resting, that was a joke! She had had only four small, very small, bit parts in the previous two years.

He, funny she always seemed to think of him as he now, not William which was his name, or Bob as his male mates called him, or Bobby which he had liked Hazel to call him. He had come to the club that first night they met with the rest of the winning rugby team. He was loud that evening, but then so were the rest of the team, but he caught her eye. He really looked good, six feet two inches tall, blond hair, deeply tanned with none of the bumps and bruises that a lot of rugby players have. His slightly heavy body shown off by the fairly light cream coloured trousers, white open necked shirt and navy blue blazer he wore, Hazel had really fancied him then, but the club was busy and they didn't get much time to talk. When the club closed, the manager had called taxis to take the team to their homes as nobody was in a fit state to drive, but Bobby had decided to stop the night. Next morning when she had come into work at 10 o'clock she was surprised to find him waiting in the car park, looking none the worse for all the drink he had taken the night before. 'Excuse me, Hazel isn't it?' her heart skipped a beat, 'the manager tells me that after your lunchtime shift you have the rest of the day off, I wonder if you would like to have dinner with me this evening?'

'Yes, that would be nice,' she answered. The fact that he was standing next to his bright red Morgan sports car had helped her make her mind up quickly.

He picked her up later at her digs saying, 'You look absolutely beautiful, I know a lovely little place about forty miles away, where the food's out of this world, are you game?' She was glad that she'd had her hair cut in the short bob style that was fashionable that year, so it didn't get blown about too much in the fast car drive. Was he trying to impress her? He was right, the food was wonderful and two other things did impress her, the fact that he didn't have a drop to drink saying, 'I never drink when I have a lovely lady like you Hazel, to drive home' and the fact he just dropped a handful of notes on the table when it was time to go, without even looking at the bill. What a charmer he was in those days.

So the courtship began. He was able to spend a lot of time with her and a lot of money on her. He worked for a London stockbroker and had been doing wonderfully well. Money was coming in hand over fist. Everything he touched turned to gold, every share he brought went up in price, making money for both his clients and himself and he only needed to work three days a week.

After five months he asked her to marry him, she said yes. Even then she knew she didn't really love him, fancied him, yes, enjoyed his company, yes, but loved him, no and was seduced by his money, his car, his good looks. He was as good as she was going to get and she couldn't understand why she didn't love him. But she knew she didn't. Two months later they were wed. The wedding was quite small, he had no relations at all, she had just her mother and father and the rest of the wedding party was made up of some people from his office, the rugby team and a few friends she had in the acting world.

The honeymoon was a shock to her; they had gone to Jamaica for three weeks. It was there she knew she had made a mistake in marrying him and that as far as he was concerned she was just another 'show', the good looking actress to be seen on his arm. Along with his Rolex watch, his sports car, his expensive clothes and the deep tan, which she found out, came from a sunbed, as he hated the sun and sand. 'But why come to Jamaica?' Hazel had asked.

'Because it's the place to be seen this year!' what a vain man he was 'and of course the casinos.' From the first day they had arrived he had gone to the casinos from about three in the afternoon until three or four in the morning, when he woke her for fast sex of the 'wham, bam thank you mam' kind, with no thought of pleasing her, falling asleep afterwards and sleeping until noon. More fast sex, shower, food and then back to the casino. She spent her time on the lovely beaches and sight-seeing, but she was lonely. Was this what marriage was all about?

His luck held and he won a very large amount, enough to pay cash for a large seven-bedroomed house in Surrey on returning to England. A three quarters of a million pound house that she was expected to look after with the held of a live-in housekeeper and a three days a week cleaner from the nearby village.

Then after about two years Hazel noticed that he was drinking heavily, was bad tempered most of the time and was putting on weight. He had given up rugby because of a knee injury and the only exercise he had was one or maybe two games of golf a week at the expensive club that was nearby.

After another year the bubble burst, as all bubbles do! He was driving home from the office, a small child ran into the road and because he had been drinking he was too slow in hitting the brake pedal. The child was killed and he lost his licence for five years and was lucky not to get a prison sentence. Then he lost his position at the stockbroking firm. He told her the stock market had fallen, which it had, that money just wasn't there to be made anymore and that he - like a lot of other stockbrokers - was being laid off. She was told later by one of the other stockbrokers' wives that he had been gambling with some of his clients' money, something to do with 'selling short and inside dealing', he had made money while his clients lost and he was asked to resign.

He began to spend more and more time at the golf club trying to impress the rich members, whom he hoped might offer him a position. Buying them drinks, funny how rich people only seemed to buy drinks for people who were even richer than them, but were quite prepared to let lesser people buy drink after drink for them with nothing in return. Of course no one offered him employment, who wanted a slightly bent stockbroker with no driving licence?

One day he came home full of excitement, saying that the gold club was up for sale, for one and a half million pounds. He'd made a date with the bank manager for the next day. Hazel was amazed, how could he raise that kind of money? But after talks with his bank manager it turned out he could. A three quarters of a million mortgage on the house, which was now worth over the million mark, selling his beloved Morgan, his Rolex, shares he had managed to hold onto and a £500,000 loan from the bank, who couldn't lose as they held the mortgage on the house plus the deeds on the club as security for the loan. These kinds of figures scared Hazel.

At once the money started to roll in, money from the yearly membership, new younger members, the newly rich he liked to call them, from the green fees, the bar, the restaurant, from the gymnasium he had installed and money he made from the buying and selling shares from tips the members gave him, inside dealing? Yes, but this time he had no job to lose and who would know.

Hazel by now really hated him, he was drinking too much, after all it was his bar. He was obese, weighing in somewhere around the eighteen stone mark. His hair was greasy, his skin pasty, he no longer bothered with the sun lamp and worse of all to Hazel was he sweated all the time. She couldn't bear for him to touch her, not that he did anyway, their sex life was extinct.

He had to die, but how do you kill someone and not be found out? A hit-man? How do you find one? And he might be traced back to her, an accident? What kind, and could she be sure he'd die. Hazel spent many a sleepless night tossing and turning trying to think of a way and how once he was dead, she would sell up, maybe go back to acting, maybe she'd meet somebody who she'd fall in love with, maybe she'd just travel the world. Whatever she did she would have money.

Two things happened on the same day to finally show her how she could do it, she'd called on the local doctor just for a check up and after examining her, Abel Seaman the doctor who was also a member of the golf club had said, 'Hazel you're in excellent health, I wish I could say the same about your husband. Please see if you can talk him into coming in to see me, you must know Hazel, he's a prime target for a heart attack. He's very much overweight, drinks too much, eats too much, he doesn't exercise at all, he no longer even plays golf. Talk to him, get him to come and see me.' Hazel had left the doctors, thinking, *talk to him!* What good would that do, he only did what he wanted to do anyway, she wished he would have a heart attack.

That same evening Hazel was leafing through a cheap woman's magazine that the cleaner had left behind. One item caught her eyes, it said that three out of five men who had heart attacks while making love, were having sex with someone other than their wives. This got Hazel thinking, *a heart attack while having sex! A heart attack from over eating, what about one caused from both or either.* Well he wasn't having sex with anybody, she was sure of this, he was at the club until it closed at midnight, a taxi home and to bed after a couple of more drinks, asleep as soon as his head hit the pillow and snored all night until between ten and eleven the next morning.

How she had hated hearing that loud snore as she laid in her own bed, they now had single beds, Hazel wanted separate rooms but hadn't as yet found a way to suggest it.

The morning after reading the magazine Hazel had woken him early, well early for him, about nine o'clock, saying she had cooked him breakfast, something she hadn't done for years, he usually had something at the club.

'Why, you haven't cooked my breakfast for years,' he asked crossly.

'Well Bobby,' she said, she hadn't called him Bobby for years. 'Our marriage is a mess, we've drifted apart, maybe it's my fault, I want us to try again and a nice breakfast cooked by me in the morning is the first step.' He had looked at her strangely, but never the less got up and came downstairs where she served him a very large fried breakfast swimming in grease, two eggs, bacon, mushrooms and fried bread. Too much for most men but being the greedy pig he was he ate it all, even thanking her afterwards. He went back upstairs to shower and was really surprised while showering Hazel had slipped into the shower cabinet naked, again a thing that hadn't happened for years, and began soaping him. He was surprised how quickly he became roused. 'Come on Bobby make love to me, it's been too long.' He did puffing and panting all the while and quickly finishing.

When he left for the club a little later she whispered in his ear, 'I enjoyed that, why don't you slip back for a while this afternoon and maybe we can carry on.' She hated the thought and as soon as he left she rushed upstairs for a shower to try and get the smell and feel of him off her.

That afternoon he did slip back, ringing her beforehand to let her know he was on his way. Knowing he would she had given the housekeeper the afternoon off, she met him in the hallway, wearing an almost transparent negligee, passed him a large whisky, 'Drink this Bobby and then let's go upstairs.' He almost ran up the stairs where he quickly had sex, she coaxed him into a second time that afternoon, then a third, something he had never managed before. That night when he came home she was waiting with a large supper, he ate it saying, 'I like the new you, what are you trying to do? Fatten me up for the kill!' If only he knew. Then more sex, she put on the show of her life, pretending that she was loving it. After this any acting she did would be easy.

This pattern went on for the next two months, he put on even more weight, he huffed and puffed even more, but no heart attack. Hazel began to wonder, was it going to work? But now she had started she had to carry on till the end.

Hazel tempted him every way she knew, bought sex books and videos and dressed up for him with clothes from the sex shop in the nearby town, nurses' uniforms, school girls' uniforms, leather wear and rubber cat suits with holes cut out. He was now having sex morning, afternoons and night, always before or after a heavy meal. He couldn't understand what was happening but he was loving it.

One afternoon when they were having sex (Hazel could never think of it as making love), he was on top, puffing and pounding away, he suddenly gave a great groan, arched up above her, then fell heavily on her, he was dead, she had finally done it! As he fell, his massive chest and weight had hit her face breaking her nose, she tried to push him off, she couldn't move him even enough to breathe, he was smothering her, she was fighting for air, she couldn't get any, she was dying. Her last thought was, *what verdict would the inquest be, murder? Suicide? Or?*

Then there was nothing.

TIMESLIP
David Spanton

Of course I didn't believe in the Supernatural. Ghosts, spirits and the like were for kids, and those who were easily scared. We lived on a planet, in a solar system, in a galaxy, which was part of an explainable, naturally occurring universe. Anything else was for those with vivid imaginations, who were easily frightened.

Then came the December night I had worked late; being the last to leave my workplace in an insurance office block. This, in the centre of a small town, on England's south coast. I left by a door, which was tucked away in the yard at the rear of the premises. It was dark, dismal and deserted, as I made sure that the door was securely fastened and the premises, therefore, safe for the night. Heavy rain was falling, and the wind, howling, was blowing a gale. I pulled the collar of my coat up around my ears and jammed my hat firmly onto the top of my head. I crossed the yard and finding my way along the wet wall to the gap in construction that was the rear entry to the site, I turned left towards the spot where my car was parked.

As I peered through the raindrops trying to keep my footing on the slippery path, I glanced up. My heart jumped and my whole body started to shake at the sight before me. We were fully two hundred yards from the seashore, but, rearing up in front of me; about, it seemed to hit me, was the hull of a large, old-fashioned sailing ship. The vessel was listing to one side and appeared to be almost waterlogged. However, the misty, rainy atmosphere seemed to clear, for just a time. I could then see the ashen faces of the two people; a man and a woman, who were leaning over the side. They looked straight at me, their mouths agape. No doubt they were calling for help. Any sound that might have been heard was whipped away by the howling wind. The ship was so close to me that I, involuntarily, took two or three steps backwards. As I did so, my hand came up in front of my face, in a half defensive, half disbelieving gesture. My eyes closed and when they opened again, the horrific vision had gone. It was still raining and the wind was still howling, but, in front of my eyes was now the usual sight of the town centre. I made my way home to my bachelor flat in the town, hardly daring to close my eyes for fear of the vision's return.

With the next day, Saturday, being a non-working day, it did not matter so much, that I found it difficult to sleep that night!

I mentioned my experience to no one; fearing what they might think, and say. I was not locally born, having been given the opportunity of a more senior employment position by my employers, which involved my moving away from a big city to a town branch. Instead, I continued with my daily routine. In time the memory of my experience faded to the back of my mind. The experience did, however, set me to question my view of a strictly material universe. If there was any reality, or explanation, to what I had seen, it did not seem to lie, in a 'nuts and bolts' existence. I felt, now, that there must be something more to our earthly existence, than I had previously thought. I had always been the first to scoff, at any religious talk, or talk, in fact, of anything else behind our lives. I was now more cautious.

I tried to play Devil's Advocate, in my own mind; endeavouring to make the experience fit into my otherwise simple view of the 'human condition'. However, I had to widen my sphere of belief to allow myself to, in some way, set my mind at ease. I enrolled, at the public library. I read books on religion and pseudo-religious beliefs. I admitted to myself that, if I abandoned a wholly materialistic view of the world, and our universe, I might, hopefully, find some way to rationalise the happenings of that night. However, my conversion was a very slow process indeed!

A year passed; I still had told no one of my experience. However, as I settled more into the community, I was, at last, given an inkling of the truth behind what I had seen. As with many such organisations, the company for which I worked encouraged their staff to join together in various outside activities. This, it was felt, would foster business activity. There was a 'formation dancing' section and on the 'sports' side, as well as the usual football and cricket teams, there was encouragement to take part in many locally organised groups for various pastimes.

It was at the end of the 'social', tagged on to a mixed darts evening, involving staff from other organisations, that a possible explanation of what lay behind my experience, presented itself. I overheard a conversation that went as follows:

First Speaker (Male): 'Of course there was no town, as such, then. It was just a fishing village and, the er, actual waterline, was farther inland than it is now. In fact, where we are standing would have been under several feet of water.'

Second Speaker (Female): 'Go on? You'll be saying there were smugglers and pirates next.'

First Speaker: 'Well, I don't know about that. However, before this land was reclaimed from the sea, there was a 'bay', and the, er, Promontory's that is the part sticking out into the sea . . .'

Second Speaker: 'OK, OK, I'm not that daft; I know what a promontory is.'

First Speaker: 'Good, then, as I say, both promontories, at each end of the bay were rocky and perilous to passing vessels.'

Second Speaker: 'Go on; pull the other one; er, I expect you were a lifeboatsman or something, eh?'

First Speaker: 'No, no, this is way before my time. But, my grandfather, who told me about it; he was attached to the coastguards. Er; they were responsible for the warning lights, and such, you know?'

Second Speaker: 'Yes, yes, come on cut to the action. You've got my interest now.'

First Speaker: 'Right, well, as I say, the tidal waters came right in, then, to cover the land we're standing on.'

Second Speaker: 'The reclaimed land?'

First Speaker: 'Yes, there were two survivors, a man and a woman, er, they were lucky enough to be in the fore part of the ship when she struck the main rocks. They were thrown clear, er, onto a dry part of the rocks.'

Second Speaker: 'And the other's on board; the ship, itself?'

First Speaker: 'Only two survivors, as I say; the ship broke up very quickly, after impacting the rocks.'

I turned away, stifling my open mouth. It seems that I had, somehow, had a vision of this occurrence. I said nothing; but came away from the social occasion with my mind, at last to a great extent, set at ease. It seems that the duo I had glimpsed, were the survivors

I still never told my tale. But, I am old now; I feel I must put details of my experience on record . . .

THE GARDEN GATE
M C Jones

The breeze came in from the western approaches and brought rain to the highlands and islands. The scudding clouds raced across the hills, their shadows running overground as they disappeared to haunt the valleys. Towns and villages nestled in the snowy mountains, dense with fog, strange accents and voices. The people were traditional, old in their ways and very, very Scottish

At the cottage, the little garden gate was open and someone was on the phone, in the kitchen. A dog was missing in the hills and there was a search party out from the neighbouring village - he had been held in great affection by the community.

'He's there somewhere,' said the owner.

'We'll find him,' said the others, although not in so many words.

Outside it was afternoon and evening very quickly and the skies closed in as the sun went down. The night stretched overhead like a horoscope, with all the stars in their places, glistening with philosophical meaning.

Something rustled in the ferns and the heathers down below. Flecks of white appeared in the dusk and a little bark was suddenly audible across the landscape. The West Highland terrier was alive and kicking although it was tired and lost as the daylight ran out. He came to a stop by a small copse and lay down for a while, panting for breath as he did so. Then, descended from wolves, he stood up, sniffed the air and raced downhill towards the cottage. He knew by instinct where to go, which pathway to follow and so on, and it wasn't very long before he was home. Dashing through the gate to a cheer from the search party, he was once again safe and sound.

The phone went down inside the house and the owner welcomed his terrier back with tea, biscuits and a sigh of relief.

'You know, that's how I feel,' said his wife, once they had shut the gate and secured the dog.

'About what?' asked the owner.

'About home, family, Scotland - everything . . . I like peace and quiet, safe haven. This place has been a sanctuary for me. I suppose I believe in the garden gate - family values, that sort of thing.'

The dog stirred by the fireside as the two adults discussed their children and their lives. Outside, the rain came down and pretty soon the windows cried in the darkness. The cottage was buffeted by the elements and they retired early to bed to escape the furore. It was a restless night until morning broke many hours later with a broad, blue sky smiling overhead.

At dawn, the storm abated and the airs and the waters stilled as the landscape calmed steadily down. The rivers flowed in the glens, the trees sang with birds and the towns came gradually to life.

'And how are we this fine Scottish morning?' asked the householder of his wife. There was a knock at the door and a chink of glass as the milkman made his delivery. He had a cheery wave to go with his job and somehow the things he said epitomised the time of day. The morning arrived with the milk float every time . . .

The west highland terrier slowly struggled to his feet once again, a little later than usual after his adventure in the hills. Scratching and sniffing, cleaning his paws and barking as he shook himself awake, he went pad, pad, pad around the kitchen and over to the front door. The newspaper was protruding through the letterbox and he took it in his jaws and pulled it angrily through until it dropped onto the doormat. He sniffed at the door again, blinked and said 'Woof,' as his master came down the stairs. It's a big job being a terrier.

'Now then, hound, don't you get too noisy. People are still getting up,' said the householder.

The little dog was his pride and joy. he was an off-white colour, though they had rubbed chalk into his fur every year to enhance the whiteness. He was small but courageous and less than ten years old, well trained and fairly well behaved, although he could be a little aggressive like all terriers.

Time passed over the cottage and the owners walked away their retirement years in the glens and by the seashores. The dog was often with them, scampering over stones and growling at the waves. If they called his name he quickened his pace to snap at their heels, shadowing their every step. He gave them a sense of tranquillity - homeliness or domesticity if you like. They joked about the black and white whisky label and often drank it on a Sunday night. Two little dogs of opposing colours play a starring role on the label, as the world knows. It was theirs. The terrier played in the sun and when it rained, hid by the fire, asleep by the warmth of a Scottish hearth. The years went by and the dog lived out his lifespan of seventeen years, slowing down as he grew older and going into a sad decline, before becoming one of the clouds in the sky.

Down in the local school, all the children of the village were sat attentively at their desks and the teacher was talking at length. 'Now the next question you're to answer is a little more complex than those you have seen before. Let's read it together, shall we?'

The boys and girls read through the essay question carefully. Someone stifled a yawn as yet another lesson in the day began. They had one hour to respond in their own words to the following:

'There is a close similarity between the concepts of imagery and metaphor. However, the two are distinct principles which stand in their own right in the English language. Explain the difference between the two in detail.'

The kids bowed their heads, pens poised at the top of the page and started to write . . .

ALBERT'S HOUSE
Sam McLean

Albert Penfold was not too happy about sharing his home with total strangers. Unfortunately, however, he had no say in the matter. Since his wife Mable passed away three years ago, his eldest daughter Catherine had dealt with all his affairs. It was her decision to rent out the house to a young couple Donald Henderson and Fiona Wakefield on a short stay basis with a view of selling the property at a later stage.

Eighty-seven year old Albert Penfold and his lovely wife Mable had lived at 24 Ribblesdale Cottage in the picturesque Northamptonshire village of Tippington for well over 60 years.

Albert, inherited the old stone built house from his great Aunt Martha. He was immediately struck by its elegant rustic charm, the warmth and beautiful simplicity of the cottage, the low ceiling with their exposed oak beams, the large open fireplace with freshly chopped logs inviting to be lit.

It had a unique and welcoming atmosphere. Albert and Mable soon fell in love with 24 Ribblesdale Cottage and the beautiful surrounding Northamptonshire countryside.

Tippington village boasts a modest population of only 432 inhabitants, resting snugly between Oundle and Thrapston close to the River Nene.

The village is steeped in history, less than half a mile from the magnificent 16 Century Tippington Hall, the ancestral home of the Seymour family.

Situated in the heart of Northamptonshire, Tippington Hall is a splendid Elizabethan mansion built in 1567 by Sir Hector Manton, a distant cousin of the Seymours.

It was once rumoured, in 1605, that Edward Seymour was one of the co-conspirators, along with Thomas Tresham, Robert Catesby and Guy Fawkes to blow up the houses of Parliament, in what became known as the 'powder treason', the gun powder plot.

This however could never be proved and unlike Guy Fawkes he managed to escape a most painful and unpleasant death.

Albert's house is one of a row of four, built in the early part of the 1800s it was originally part of the Seymour estate.

The cottages were used to accommodate workers and their families employed in service at Tippington Hall.

In the late 1830s a young and very attractive housemaid by the name of Martha Cunningham was working for Lord Seymour. She had a secret and illicit affair with his youngest son, Cedric the Third Earl of Tippington. This resulted in Martha becoming pregnant with his child.

Martha and Cedric, although deeply in love and devoted to one another, knew their relationship could never develop and flourish.

There was a wide difference in both their class and background. They were reluctantly forced to end their relationship.

To avoid scandal, Martha was given 24 Ribblesdale Cottage by the Seymour family on condition she remained silent about the affair, never to mention that Cedric Seymour was the father of her unborn child.

Heartbroken at the loss of her love for Cedric she vowed never to marry. True to her word, she remained a spinster until her death aged 92.

When Albert Penfold moved into Aunt Martha's house with his lovely young wife Mable they discovered, hidden in a small leather box next to the dressing table, an old photograph of a young handsome Cecil Seymour, together with a small number of love letters from him to his beloved Martha. They were neatly folded and wrapped in fine silk, tied with a pale blue ribbon bearing the Seymour emblem.

Albert and Mable silently read the beautifully hand-written letters and were saddened at Aunt Martha's lost love.

In all the letters, Cedric stresses his love and devotion for Martha. He is beside himself with grief at the end of their relationship, wishing things could have been so different between them.

In his final letter to Martha he says his last goodbye, saying he will treasure the times they spent together, wishes her well for the future.

By all accounts their lives went in different directions, their paths never again to cross.

Several months later, however, Albert was to discover a more sinister find. While clearing out the cellar he stumbles across a number of small wooden cases, on opening one, he is horrified to discover the mummified remains of two small baby boys.

Were these the children of Cecil Seymour and his great aunt Martha Cunningham?

He is mystified at how and why they died.

Albert immediately informs his wife Mable of his gruesome discovery. After a lot of soul searching, they decide not to inform the authorities.

They did not wish to betray Aunt Martha's secret.

Instead, they buried the bodies of the two small babies in the cellar of 24 Ribblesdale Cottage.

Over the next 60 years Albert and Mable live relatively happy in the house, raising a family of three, Simon, Angela and Catherine.

The children were never informed of Aunt Martha's secret. Albert and Martha never discussed it with them.

The children were however, discouraged from going into the cellar. The door was always kept locked.

Only Simon, Albert's 16-year-old son chose to ignore his father's advice, three days later his body was found floating in the swollen River Nene, close to Ribblesdale cottage, he had apparently tragically drowned in a fishing accident.

So, to the present day, and to the young couple Donald Henderson and Fiona Wakefield being shown around the house by Albert's eldest daughter Catherine. They have no knowledge of the history and dark secrets of 24 Ribblesdale Cottage. Albert is eager to keep it that way.

Over the coming months Albert did everything in his power to persuade this young couple to leave his beloved house, he found their presence intrusive and most unwelcome, he feared the day they would enter the cellar and unleash the dark secrets that lay there. He didn't wish the past to be disturbed.

So from the moment Donald and Fiona moved into Albert's house, he set about his task and objective to have them removed.

He was however, only too aware of his limitations. He knew he wouldn't be capable of physically throwing them out of his beloved home. So to be successful, he would have to be more devious and cunning.

He set about his plan to come between them, to get them fighting and squabbling among themselves. In a word, to cause the maximum friction.

Most of the time Albert would keep a low profile, staying out of the way in his room. Only occasionally venturing out into other parts of the house when he knew his unwelcome quests were out of the way.

Albert liked nothing more than to relax quietly in his favourite leather chair in front of a large open fire and reminisce. All the happy contented memories he had collected and stored during his 60 years at 24 Ribblesdale cottage had built up and generated an array of positive psychic energy. He would sit for hours mesmerised by the flickering flames of the open log fire.

Only to have his peace and quiet abruptly disturbed, by the return of Donald and Fiona. His nasty unpleasant, unwelcome quests.

On entering the cottage Fiona would be heard to complain of the faint smell of pipe tobacco constantly present in the main lounge. Despite opening the windows to let in fresh air, and regularly spraying the room with air freshener, the smell of stale tobacco would constantly linger.

Albert liked his pipe. Now he knew it annoyed his daughter's guests he would smoke even more.

One day Donald and Fiona had been out shopping. Fiona bought herself an expensive, fine cut glass flower vase, placing it on her bedroom window. The next day Albert entered the room and wickedly unhooked the latch, allowing the strong wind to blow open the window knocking the vase to the ground, smashing it into a thousand pieces.

Fiona was most upset, and angrily blamed Donald for not closing the window correctly.

Donald strenuously denied that he had touched the window. They argued for days, much to the amusement of Albert.

His scheme was beginning to bear fruit. Over the coming months he continued to quietly cause havoc and mayhem, playing on the emotions of Donald and Fiona.

Personal items like earrings, broaches etc, even car keys would go missing, only to mysteriously reappear several days later in some other part of the house.

Once again the mischievous Albert, was responsible.

After several more months of living at 24 Ribblesdale Cottage, the relationship between Donald and Fiona was becoming more strained and agitated. Constantly at each other's throats, in what appeared to be petty and insignificant issues.

Albert's presence was having its desired effect. He was succeeding in forming a wedge between Donald and Fiona. He believed he was getting close to his objective. Soon they would part, leaving him in peace.

On Donald's 23rd birthday, Fiona decided to cook a special romantic candlelit dinner for two. With champagne, accompanied by quiet seductive background music, she wanted to create the mood for a night of love and passion.

During the meal they laughed and giggled like teenagers in love, Fiona mentioned all the strange, unexplained happenings that had taken place since they arrived at Ribblesdale Cottage. Jokingly commenting, *'There must be a ghost in the house.'* They both laughed loudly, shrugging off the suggestion.

During conversation, Donald remarked he had found the missing key to the cellar, and in the morning he was going to explore.

They finished their meal. Grabbed hold of two glasses and the remains of the champagne, arm in arm they climbed the dark narrow staircase to the master bedroom.

It was mid-winter, the bedroom felt damp and cold, Donald lit the gas fire to warm the room before they snuggled between the sheets to make love.

The bodies of Donald and Fiona were found next morning by Albert's daughter Catherine. She found them dead in bed, still embraced in each other's arms.

At the inquest into the tragic deaths of Donald Henderson and Fiona Wakefield the Coroner Martin Cromwell recorded a verdict of accidental death from Monoxide poisoning due to a faulty gas fire.

We know better, don't we!

DEATH COMES LIKE A THIEF IN THE NIGHT - TWICE?
Gerard Allardyce

There was a grey sky oppressing the sea and Cornish coastline that was Crackington Haven. It was raining slightly. The year was 1958 and I was six years of age. I was on holiday with my parents and they were taking me to the parish church of Crackington Haven. It was the first day of our holiday and Dad was looking forward to a restful break from the office. Dad had left the car, a Singer, in the town car park and as we entered the grounds of the church through the lych gate, Mum was carrying some beautiful lilies.

'Doris is buried in this part of the cemetery,' she said to my father. Dad felt suitably concerned and held my hand tightly.

'Your cousin is buried here Gerard and she is now in Heaven,' Dad said and there was quite a degree of seriousness in his voice.

Mother found the grave and we all joined her. The cross that marked the grave was Celtic-shaped.

'I like the Celtic Cross,' Dad said to my mother. 'Celtic Crosses can be found thousands of miles away, in fact as far as India.'

'This is probably the first bunch of flowers laid on Doris' grave since she died in 1929 . . . poor Doris.' As she spoke a weak sun shone through the clouds. It was difficult to believe it was July and the height of the summer.

'Can I go looking for shells in the rockpools tomorrow Dad?'

'I'll have to see about that Gerard. Let's wait to see how the weather turns out.'

Dad was always a cautious man who worked out the pros and cons of anything very carefully. It was only thirteen years since the war and Dad was 30% war disabled and received a pension accordingly. How he often wished for the return of his days in the services before the war . . . sun-drenched beaches in Alexandria and carefree days in bases in the Sudan, working only three hours of the morning and playing games in the afternoon. Now he was tied to a desk in an office he hated. The pilgrimage to the church and cemetery where my cousin was laid to rest was at an end.

'Can you swim Daddy?'

'Of course Daddy can swim. He was one of the best in the squadron Gerard,' my mother replied.

My father drove my mother and I back to the guest house where we were staying, a short distance away from the church on the cliff top. Dad was so pleased with his black and green saloon car. The manufacturer had been the same as that of the Singer sewing machine company.

The next day was cloudy and overcast and there was rain in the air.

'Can I go looking for shells on the beach, Dad?' I asked in a kind of way that no doubt was a method of attracting sympathy.

'Of course you can. We will all go to the beach in Crackington Haven to see if we can find some shells. Perhaps if you are successful in your search, you can take some shells back to school with you.'

'Perhaps the weather will buck up Gerard. I'll ask Mrs Williams if she can make us a flask of tea and some sandwiches.'

'May I have some eggy boys . . . ?'

'I'm sure that will be all right Gerard,' Mum replied happily . . .

Not only did Mrs Williams make a flask of tea and prepare some sandwiches, for some reason she went into the car park and waved us goodbye.

It was about 10 o'clock when we arrived at the beach. Dad had decided he would read The Guardian newspaper sitting on the bench overlooking the beach on the cliff top. Mother and I went down onto the beach and I started looking for colourful shells in the rockpools with a little net.

Dad was absorbed reading the newspaper. The Financial Secretary to the Treasury, a certain Mr Enoch Powell had given a glowing report on the British economy, in particular, car manufacture. The country was just picking up after the austerity of the years of a Labour government after the war.

I had seen a shell at the bottom of a rockpool and I was keen to fish it out. My legs were astride the pool. My mother was watching the incoming waves crash onto the beach and felt the rain falling in the wind. I slipped and fell into the rockpool.

Dad had decided he had had enough reading the newspaper and had come down the concrete steps to the beach. He saw my mother and knew instinctively something was wrong:

'Where's Gerard?' he asked my mother.

'I think he has fallen into a rockpool . . .' she replied in a way that gave rise to every anxiety.

It was nearly 30 years ago on a different day further up the coast on a beach bathed in sunshine and a sky so very blue that three people sat in deckchairs.

Uncle James and his wife Aunt Anne were with their only daughter Doris. She was their pride and joy, a fetching young lady of 21 in skin-tight swimsuit and skull cap.

'Do have a cup of tea before you go for a swim Doris.'

'All right Daddy,' she replied. She loved her father and there was a strong bonding between father and daughter. Aunt Anne gave her a tomato and ham sandwich and then offered her a Cornish pastie.

'Oh no Mummy. I'll have the sandwich but not the pastie, too much indigestion.'

Uncle James admired his daughter, standing as she was near the seashore. She had obtained a first class Classics degree from Oxford University just like himself. Uncle James had a swimming blue just like his daughter . . . she was ready for a swim.

'I'll be only 20 minutes,' she said in a jovial fashion.

He watched her swim out far to sea and then 35 minutes went by and looking out to sea saw an arm hanging out of the water in distress. Without giving his wife a by your leave he was in the water heading out on the long journey nearly three miles after her and like the faithful father he was, he reached her. There was no time to check whether she was alive or dead. He just felt he had to get her back to shore and to her mother.

When he reached the shore he was totally exhausted and the local coastguard was there to render assistance. Doris was adjudged to be dead by drowning. Barely a year later Uncle James had died from tuberculosis said to have been caused by that Herculean swim, a forlorn bid to save his darling daughter's life.

Thirty years later, my father was stumbling over the rocks on the Cornish beach trying to find me and he heard my cries. I was up to my neck in water, in this very small rockpool.

'Come on Gerard, take hold of my hands,' and then when I gripped his hands Dad also slipped and fell into the pool, but I could not have been in a very deep pool with a more capable person. Within just a minute I was out of the pool and so was Dad and with Mum the three of us made for the steps up the cliff face and to the car park. Dad was not very pleased because as he said to my mother, he was sopping wet.

When we arrived at the guest house Mrs Williams was delighted to see us and concerned about our clothes which were suitably washed and dried. Dad had a whisky that night suitably arranged by Mrs Williams, but all was well.

WILL CINDERS
Joyce Walker

Not long ago, in a town not so very far away, lived a young man named Will Cinders.

Will lived with his father and two brothers in a house in the suburbs and spent most of his time looking after them because his mother, unable to tolerate his father's drunkenness had run off with the milkman and left them to fend for themselves.

Every Saturday and Sunday he would be forced to stay at home and do the household chores while the other members of the family went off to watch the local team play football. The nearest he got to the pitch was watching Match of the Day, when they were drinking in the pub at night.

Will loved football, he'd excelled at it at school, and his one wish was to play on the hallowed turf at Wembley.

'Some chance of that,' he muttered to himself, as he took out his too small, worn out boots and old school strip. 'Even if I had time to play on a Saturday between all the shopping, cleaning and ironing, no team would have me wearing these old rags.'

You can imagine Will's misery when Cup Final day arrived and his father and brothers, who had talked of nothing else since they'd managed to get tickets, went off to London without him, leaving him with nothing but a broken television set for company.

He was just about to take it to pieces and see if he could mend it when there was a knock at the door.

Visitors to the house were rare and he had never before seen the man who stood on his doorstep, so he asked, 'Who are you?'

'I am your fairy goalkeeper,' the man replied, 'and I've come to grant your wish.'

Will eyed him suspiciously, 'Right now, all I want is a TV repair man. I don't suppose you're any good with televisions?'

'No, but I do know that New Town United need a centre forward and I can get you there in time to play.'

Will didn't believe the man at all, but he let him into the house anyway. Any kind of company was better than none.

Once inside, the man looked about him, 'Well, there's not much to work from,' he mumbled, 'but we'll have to do the best we can. First bring me your old football strip and boots, if you're going to play, you need to look the part.'

Deciding the man was a nutcase who needed humouring, Will did as he was told. 'Put them over the back of the chair and say the magic words with me.'

'What magic words?' Will asked.

'The final score of today's match,' said his fairy goalkeeper. 'One nil, but you must repeat it several times, or the spell won't work.'

So the two men stood together and chanted over and over, 'One nil, one nil, one nil, one nil, one nil . . .' Suddenly there was a sound like thunder and a cloud of smoke filled the room. When it cleared, there on the chair lay the peacock blue and white strip of New Town United and on the floor beside it a pair of shiny black football boots.

Will couldn't believe what he was seeing. He blinked hard a couple of times, then closed his eyes very tightly, thinking that when he opened them he'd be alone in the room with the broken TV set. When he unclenched his lids the blue and white strip was still there and so was the funny little man.

'You really are my fairy goalkeeper!' he exclaimed.

'Yes, and there's not a moment to lose, you've already missed the team coach, I'll have to think of another way to get you there.' He played with the whiskers on his chin, a gesture showing he was deep in thought, but not for long. 'Get me one of those empty lager cans you were saving to take to the recycling bank.'

Will, now he believed, responded quickly to the request.

'Oh dear, the garden's a bit small, isn't there anywhere bigger?'

'There's the school playing field at the back, we can climb over the hedge,' Will replied obligingly.

They took the can to the centre of the field and Will's fairy goalkeeper led him to stand as far away from it as was possible.

'We'll need some really powerful magic for this one,' he said. 'I hope you know the Liverpool anthem.'

The two men joined in chorus with each other and as their voices reached a crescendo with the words, *and you'll never walk alone,* there was another really loud clap of thunder, followed by a flash of bright lightning and a thick blanket of smoke.

When it cleared, standing before him complete with pilot, was a helicopter. Will's fairy goalkeeper handed him a sports bag containing his kit. 'Go,' he shouted, then, 'wait, before you do, there is one word of warning. You must be back by five or your beautiful new strip will turn back into your old one and you'll look really stupid.'

Will thanked the man profusely, and ducking his head under the rotor blades, ran to the helicopter.

Twenty minutes later he was on the pitch, lined up with the other players, waiting for a good luck wish from the royal visitor who would later present the cup.

He looked about him at the spectators, trying to catch a glimpse of his father and brothers, but there were so many faces it was impossible to distinguish theirs from the rest.

Will loved the monarchy almost as much as he loved football and of all the royals the one he loved the most was Princess Charmayne. She was young and beautiful, what's more, she loved football, so it should have been no surprise to him to see her standing there, her pale blue eyes staring into his, wishing him well for the coming game.

He felt a sudden stirring in his loins and his heart was still pounding when the whistle sounded for the kick-off.

The first half was unspectacular, a few missed chances on both sides, the odd foul, and the teams still tied at 0-0 when the first forty-five minutes was over.

They started the second half with all to play for and both teams tried their hardest to succeed. There were a few corner kicks, none of which were converted into goals, a few blatant attempts by players to try and force a penalty by throwing themselves down in the area at the slightest knock from an opposing player, all refused by the referee. With less than a minute of extra time to go it looked like there might have to be a replay.

This worried Will, for there was probably no way he would be able to make the team again. A huge problem, demanding drastic action. He passed three players with lightning speed to get to the ball that was now high in the air. He had never been good at headers, there was only one thing for it. He did a back-flip, and in a style not witnessed since the playing days of Pele, gave an overhead kick that sent the ball flying into the back of the net. The whistle sounded and New Town United had won the FA Cup.

Will, the conquering hero, was carried on shoulders to the foot of the grandstand to mount the steps ahead of everyone and collect the trophy from his beloved princess.

In the melee that followed he forgot all about his fairy goalkeeper and the five o'clock warning. He'd exchanged shirts with an opposing player and was posing for photographs when the clock began to strike, only then did he remember and as the shirt in the player's hand turned to rags, he ran out of the stadium and along the road to the nearest bus stop.

One of his bootlaces had come undone and in his rush to get away he had no time to fasten it and no time to pick up the boot when it came off at the bottom of the VIP stand.

For days afterwards the papers were full of the mysterious player who had come in at short notice to replace the injured centre forward. There were rumours that the princess had kept the football boot as a souvenir and was anxious to trace the man it belonged to.

Rumours that were later proved true, when the princess herself came on TV and radio with the announcement that she would take whoever the boot fitted, away to the Caribbean islands for a holiday. She would, of course, be on hand to whisk away the lucky man, as soon as he was found.

Fittings were arranged at New Town Town Hall and every male in the surrounding district, queued for days to be given the chance of trying it on.

Will almost didn't go because his brothers had teased him unmercifully, saying the boot couldn't possibly fit, because he'd been at home all day, fixing the television, which incidentally, was working when he got back later on Cup Final day. Anyway, he thought, there must be loads of men in the area with a size seven foot like his.

He took his shopping list as usual and drove to the supermarket for the weekend groceries. Then, he thought, what the hell, and leaving the car in the car park, headed round the corner to join the very back of the queue.

Even though it was moving quickly, it was dark by the time he entered the hall. The princess looked him up and down, vague recognition dawning in those pale blue eyes of hers, but she said nothing, just gestured him to the chair where someone asked him to take off his trainer and try on the boot. Which of course fitted him like a . . . well, a football boot actually.

The princess was ecstatic. She gave him a very unregal hug and kiss on the mouth, to which he replied with a very sloppy one of his own, and another and another.

People cheered, reporters tried to break up the happy scene with demands for interviews, but it wasn't until much later that they pushed their way through the paparazzi and into the waiting limousine, drove off into the night and lived happily together, in sin, ever after.

MARTHA
Phyllis Spooner

I clearly recall our tutor's words to us all on the day when I and three others joined our writing class. He said that whilst the brochure had described our course as 'Writing For Pleasure And Profit', he found it only fair to warn us that whilst hopefully, we would gain pleasure from it, we certainly wouldn't become rich! This didn't deter anyone, and we still enjoy our meetings after several years. He was right about the money!

When one or two had short stories published, we were pleased for them and whilst not expecting any miracles as far as the majority of the rest of our entries was concerned, we did, nevertheless, eventually all have at least one story accepted by a woman's magazine. All, that is, except Martha.

Poor Martha, she never complained, and she suitably praised each of us as the acceptances came in. I began to think that she had never sent any stories up, for her writing was good, and that was the opinion of us all. She had a style rather like Catherine Cookson, tales of hardship. Characters jumped off the pages, so when we listened to her quiet reading voice, living the emotions of them all, we identified with each one. Martha's face though, never showed a flicker of emotion either whilst she was reading or when she spoke to us, in class or out. She was a very private person, who lived alone.

One day she read out a really superb piece called, 'The Straight And Narrow Path'. It was about a young girl who had to give up her own loves and ambitions in life to stay single and look after an aged, widowed mother. I think we all knew then what had happened in her own upbringing.

I made a point of speaking to Martha at coffee break. She looked surprised when I sat by her for she never spoke whilst she had her coffee; but she looked resigned at being disturbed. 'Martha, that was a fantastic story, what made you write it? It wasn't a set piece was it?' I knew full well it wasn't but I was conjuring up a plan to help her, as I thought, well, just to give her a push into the publishing world. I had a feeling it would work.

'No,' she answered in her quiet, monotonous tone, 'I wrote it long ago; I thought you would like to hear it instead of the last piece set, which wasn't really my style.'

'I really would love to read it again Martha, do you have a copy I could take home? I'll keep it safe.'

I fancied I caught a glimmer of pride and a slight smile from her as she handed me the story later on. I wouldn't tell a soul of my plans, of course, but if they worked, then Martha would no longer be the odd one out in our group, then maybe she would look a bit happier. I figured that her type of story would suit the older style women's magazine, so I settled for Read Weekly. I duly retyped her story, word for word; typed a front sheet and a short accompanying letter; then I did the dreaded thing of signing Martha's name and sent it off. Only when it was safely in the letter box and could not be retrieved, did I have a slight, worrying feeling about the exercise.

Three or four weeks went by and I began to forget about it, though once or twice I did feel that if Read Weekly did not accept it, it was their loss. It truly was a solid, heart-rending story. And in any case, we all knew that some of the stories published, to our minds, were complete rubbish. *Yes,* I thought, *I'm still confident they'll take it.*

Three weeks later the acceptance note plopped through my letter box. I felt like rushing round to Martha's but I knew I must wait till the magazine came out, then I could present her with it and the cheque too. Wouldn't Martha be pleased at being doubly blessed? Of course she would. So, on the fourteenth of March I trotted down to the newsagent's and bought five copies.

'Got another story in have we?' enquired the cheery shopkeeper.

'No, but a friend has,' I replied excitedly.

I realised that I would have to rush round to Martha's before anyone else did and when she answered the door I almost fell into the hall without being invited.

'Where's the fire?' she chided unsmilingly and telling me to sit down.

'I've brought you something that I hope you'll be pleased about.'

As I spoke I felt less confident that Martha was going to understand my intentions.

'Oh yes?' she questioned, as she sat down opposite me. I opened the magazine at the centre spread which was all hers. The title was in violet print, and eye-catching. Below it, laid out across the middle of the two pages stood a young girl in her teens, in Victorian clothing, standing affectionately by the side of her mother in an armchair, smoothing the pillows around her.

Martha stared in disbelief: and more so when she spotted her full name in bright green in the right-hand corner.

'I knew this was a wonderful story Martha,' I began to waffle a little. 'I wanted you to have something published as we all have, I wasn't convinced that you had sent anything away yourself, so I've given you a push.'

Martha's eyes widened and her eyebrows were raised. I couldn't believe that she wasn't metaphorically jumping for joy.

'You've given me a headache I think,' she said quietly. She went on to ask whether I had offered First British Serial Rights to Read Weekly.

'Of course,' I replied, pleased with myself. Martha groaned.

'Cheer up,' I said, 'I've also made you £250. Aren't you pleased?'

Martha left her seat and took a magazine from off the piano. I recognised it as Armchair Stories, printed in the same building as Read Weekly.

'I was going to bring this to the class tomorrow,' she said as she opened the book to page five, before handing it to me. 'I also offered First British Serial Rights to Armchair Stories for the same tale.'

It was my turn to groan now, but I turned to the story in front of me; another double spread with the title attracting the reader immediately *The Straight And Narrow Path* by Martha Francis. This time there was a different angle on the illustration. A young girl in a long, flowing dress and swinging a basket of bluebells in one hand, and carrying a posy of primroses in the other, was walking down a long, narrow pathway through a wood. There were tall trees either side.

'This is beautiful,' I said.

Martha stared at me. She didn't look so cross now; in fact, I thought she was about to smile. I was about to dismiss the idea though because I couldn't remember her smiling, when she started to really chuckle. She was a different person now from the staid lady we met each Wednesday and I liked her better. It didn't alter the fact though that I could be in trouble over this desire to help someone achieve an ambition and I asked her what I should do to make amends.

'Do I confess to the editor of Read Weekly?'

'I don't know,' she laughed again, 'we'll sleep on it and tomorrow we'll tell the group all about it and ask their advice. And Christine,' she said, 'if you have any more bright ideas, run them by me first!'

ALL ABOUT ME
Lyndsay Cox

Did you look at her? As your head lolled to one side. Did she reach out
to kiss you? . . . before you died.
This picture of you Thomas, hung high in the Tate Gallery that I stare
at. You know you're a lot like me, they say you were a genius, perhaps
a little vain. I'm a genius waiting to be discovered.

Today witness the death of a student never mind you, the dead poet.
It was mid-November and cold when you were brought into the world.
Me? I arrived in the spring of 1965.

Oh Thomas, you thought me young like you, I'm an old student and
I'm originally from Bristol too, but that's where the similarities end. I
cannot afford to learn anymore and you couldn't afford to live.

So I'll tell you my story and see what you think. I am not sure that
arsenic is the answer, but I'm on the brink of disaster. Perhaps I'm the
poet and you're the silent master? I could hear the girls calling me; well
they were hardly girls. They were in their thirties, playing at writing. I
wasn't playing. My two friends, Karen and Sandra were grinning as
they moved towards me. What did my face say? Did it betray my sour
thoughts? Did I mention their other hobbies? They include coffee
mornings, the gym, jumble sales and lost causes. They kept me in their
fold out of pity. Their husbands play golf and mow the lawn on
Sundays. I had a husband richer than theirs, richer by miles, but I was
traded in for a newer model.

'Kate,' they called in unison.

'I was just coming.' They weren't bad really.

'Come on swot, how do we handle the homework?' asked Karen.

'Yeah swot,' Sandra was like Karen's echo.

'Well I think . . .' I was cut off mid-sentence.

Karen rolled her eyes. 'Janet's gone for a latte and a biscotti thingy.'

'I like biscottis,' Sandra almost whispered.

I stood patiently, looking at their elegantly stencilled faces. I sighed
and half-turned and spoke to you, Thomas. I am sorry, but I am going to
make your life up. I turned back to them; they were waiting for me this
time.

'He's called Henry, like the painter.'

'What painter?' they chorused.

'Henry Wallis.'

'Who's he?' asked Sandra.

'The guy who did the painting and the guy in it is Henry too.' Karen offered.

Sandra nodded. 'Like a self-portrait then?'

Karen looked confused, and I looked away for what seemed ages.

'No,' Karen finally said, 'because the guy in the picture is dead, I think. So it can't be a self-portrait.'

They burst into giddy laughter.

'What do you think Kate?' asked Sandra.

'I think you should make of it what you will.'

'Mmm,' they both nodded sagely.

'Kate, what will you write? You're so good,' they seemed to chime.

Janet weaved her way towards us with her latte. *My saviour* I thought.

Their voices fell away and time lay suspended. I could see them muttering out of the corner of my eye. I could see them edging toward you Thomas, or Henry as you now were to them.

'How do you find the gallery Kate?'

'Smaller,' I laughed, 'but just as beautiful. I was sixteen last time I came here. A school field trip as they called them back then.'

Then you threw me Janet, I turned back to see your face, your reaction, for our eyes to meet. But I got the top of your head; I could see grey hairs seeping through your scalp. You were making notes. So I sat down next to you.

Then I thought about you, Thomas. Lying across your bed, the room looked comfortable you had a pot plant too, did you water it? Was it really there, perhaps Henry liked to paint plants? Your friends had eventually broken into your lodgings and found your body distorted and bloated from the convulsions it had suffered. You were scattered over your room like manuscripts across a floor. Were you with anyone? Did your talent absorb and devour your warmth? Were you frigid? That's me allegedly. Once again, my life was slipping into yours; sorry this is all about you.

Yet he told me I was a frigid cow. It was him with the wandering hands. They made my blood freeze when he touched me, where had those hands been? Running over his sun-tanned secretary's breasts?

Seventeen you were, perhaps too young to feel raw emotion. My vision blurred, and I slid back to reality. Janet was arguing at full tilt! My name, me as always was being brought into play.

'She said he was called Henry!' Sandra pouted.

Who's she? I thought . . . *the cat's mother?*

'That's the painter,' Janet said wearily.

'We know!' they said in blind determination.

'He, for the last time, is called Thomas Chatterton.'

Janet must have felt me at her side for she turned to me for help. 'Can you help your friends understand what I am saying?'

They were past help I thought. But how could I refuse her? I took a deep breath. 'Thomas Chatterton born 1752 died 1770 by his own hand, one of the original Romantics.'

'Thank you Kate, at least someone has learnt something.' In that moment the look on their faces, the look on Janet's face, it was all worth it! They looked at me but their eyes weren't full of hate, it was pity, the kind that flicked across my son's face.

'How could you?' Sandra bawled.

'What?' I said evenly. 'Make you look like a pair of superficial prats not caring two shits about your Master's degree.'

Karen pounced. 'This is all about Tim isn't it?'

'Leave my ex out of this.'

'You're jealous! Jealous we're still married. Still got men . . .' she stumbled.

Janet spoke quietly to us. 'Ladies remember where you are!'

Karen fell quiet and Sandra was like a stone statue.

We left the Tate and made our way to the Underground, we followed Janet. We didn't speak, that is until we surfaced at Marylebone Station. The feeling was suffocating, thankfully Sandra and Karen decided to stop for a bite to eat.

That just left the two of us waiting for a train to go to Chorleywood. How much could you tell a person in forty minutes? I managed quite a lot and she listened.

I didn't want to go home to my man-less life, and I wanted a son who respected me and didn't look down on me because I stacked shelves for a living. Well Thomas, was it worth it, glimpsing my life?

That's my story. I had almost forgotten about Janet as I chanted my internal thoughts. Yes son, I know where I'm going. You'll be better off with your father, he can pay for your driving lessons, I sure as hell can't afford them! What can I do? I can price up baked beans as fast as anyone. I was suddenly aware of Janet scurrying at my side. I stopped.

'Sorry, I get carried away,' I began to walk slowly.

'You're upset, anyone can see there's a lot going on in your head.'

'Understatement!' I shouted. 'For an English teacher that was the most pathetic observation I have ever heard!'

'Now just one damn minute!' Janet barked. I stopped. 'You are a rude, ungrateful cow! You can be very funny if you would just stop chewing on a wasp. Yes, your friends were cruel, but you have the intellect to be crueller and you were.'

'Yes, well thanks for your insight, I won't burden you anymore.'

'That martyr act is wearing very thin,' she added.

I slammed the car door, with Janet's voice ringing in my ears. I drove off; it had been a long day. The sun was getting ready to set. Long fingers of light spreading out like a guiding hand before me. Death was calling me, inviting me, I pressed harder on the accelerator. No, I wouldn't, that was too easy. So I slowed down and there was my home. In a hamlet of nine houses and a pub, idyllic right? I turned into my little drive and there was Oscar waiting to greet me. He wound himself between my legs and as I opened the door he leapt onto the sofa, which was bathed in golden sunlight.

I poured myself a very large glass of wine and I sat down. I opened my work and rested it on the coffee table. I kicked my shoes off and stretched out on the sofa. Out of my jeans pocket fell Janet's card with her number, when had she stuck that there?

The scene was set, I am sorry Thomas I didn't mean to offend you or betray what we had today and it had been special. I topped up my wine and took a handful of paracetamols; my head was getting heavy, lolling to one side just like yours Thomas. Blackness was coming. I did like pot plants I'm sorry Jake. Jake is my son, sorry Oscar, sorry Tim. I was too cowardly to write a note. I floated on happy thoughts then I tried to force more tablets into my mouth, but my mouth wouldn't work, they slipped out and scattered over the floor. I smiled, I could see someone, was it you Thomas? Someone was violently shaking me and throwing water on me. Was I dreaming? The cool blackness crept over my soul and all was quiet again. I was being shaken again.

'Leave me alone,' I slurred. I think it was Jake, my son. I glared, he looked a little upset; I hadn't known he was coming home for dinner. I had plenty of beans though. He was talking on the phone and reading a label, then suddenly I was wet again, more water. He kept shaking me.

'Let me die please, I can't afford driving lessons.'

He was crying, then there was another voice. God, who had he phoned? Not Tim, please not Tim.

'How many has she taken?' It was Janet's voice.

'I dunno, there are some on the floor, but she's had wine, a load of wine.'

Jake was crying, breaking his heart.

'Leave him alone and piss off! I want to die.'

'Tough!' Janet snarled back.

'Come on Jake,' Janet soothed. 'You've done OK, now go and put the kettle on there's a good lad.'

'I love her you know,' he sobbed. 'I've been a right bastard.'

'Shh now, no one need know, she won't die.'

'Proud of yourself are you?' she spoke fiercely.

I could hear her fear. 'How can I be proud, I'm not dead.'

'That's the spirit a martyr to the end.'

She pushed her hand down my throat. I wretched and began to shut my eyes. 'I promised Jake you wouldn't die.'

'I don't want to be here. I cannot do it anymore.'

She pushed her hand down my throat again. I threw up this time.

'You are such a drama queen!'

'I haven't anyone to love.'

'You have me.'

'Do I?'

'Just said so.'

Suddenly my heart knotted, it was being squeezed like a sponge. I couldn't breathe.

'Ambulance please, I think it's a heart attack.' Janet was on the phone.

I was dying? She said a heart attack, this was no way to go, I hadn't wanted this! I held Janet's hand, I was sick again.

'That's it girl, get it up.'

But the blackness came again, but this time it swallowed me whole and the light was gone. There was a silence and Janet waited, she scanned the class for a moment.

'So that was your introduction to Early Romantic seventeenth century poetry. Now go and scribble geniuses and I will see you all Monday. Oh, were there any questions?' She was bowled over by verbal cacophony.

Janet held her hand up.

'Ladies, I want you to go away and learn verisimilitude.'

HALLOWE'EN CAPERS
Cynthia Davis

Angie cast a critical eye over the contents of her bulging wardrobe. After several long minutes she opted to wear her long, black skirt with pixie boots. She had to look good tonight, it was Hallowe'en. Once dressed, she took a last look in the mirror and smiled at her reflection.

Angie raced down the stairs and with a yell of, 'Catch you later Mom,' slammed the door behind her, the clicking of her boots was the only sound to disturb the empty street. Angie glanced at her watch, it was getting late; she didn't want to keep Sharon waiting.

Her friend was already sitting on the steps of the town hall as Angie turned the corner. It was good to see the town alive with fun and laughter tonight. All the kids hanging out for a fright on Hallowe'en. The girls sat together in comfortable silence. Everyone at school thought they were sisters with their long, dark hair and impish hazel eyes. Suddenly Angie shivered with cold as from out of nowhere an icy wind blew up the alley towards them, howling like a banshee. Then just as quickly it was gone! *Was that an omen?* she wondered. Then she caught sight of Wendy and her gang heading their way. Angie's heart sank. Wendy was the school bully, she was broad as well as tall and her height gave her an advantage. She towered above all the other kids at school! Wendy liked nothing better than to bully all and sundry and because Angie was petite and doll-looking she always took a hammering! As Wendy stood over Angie who was now filled with fear as she wondered, what would Wendy do now? Her tormentor towered over her, taking in every inch of Angie's Hallowe'en gear, then with a voice filled with sarcasm and loathing she spat out the words, 'My, you look quite the witch tonight. Where have you left your broom?'

Angie felt the anger rise, but being a gentle soul she didn't retaliate. It was left to Sharon to take control. 'C'mon babe, let's hit the town,' her soothing words acting like a balm. Angie let herself be led away, but couldn't resist looking back at her enemy and noticing with some dismay, the look of triumph on her smug, round face.

All was soon forgotten as the girls passed the shop windows. It seemed as though everyone had made an effort this year, including the record shop. Angie and Sharon pressed their faces up against the window and peered inside. They were soon in awe at the sight of candlelit pumpkins that sat side-by-side on the shelves. Stuck fast to the window were fierce-looking werewolves and black, red-eyed hounds that oozed blood from their fearful fangs. As they looked in the next window their eyes were drawn to the mannequins that some wag had dressed up. They shuddered at the sight of Dracula who stood alone in the corner of the shop. Wearing a black and red cape and those dark, brooding eyes, he seemed to beckon them in. Quickly the girls looked at Frankenstein as he lay, eyes closed on a long, wooden table as though asleep for eternity. Around his head were several layers of dirty grey bandages. There was even a toothless old hag suspended from the ceiling on her broomstick. There'd be no flying for her tonight! Both girls agreed, this was the coolest shop ever. But Angie was bored, she wanted more, there had to be more than this on Hallowe'en. With a sigh she pulled out a torch from her pocket and shone it up the alley.

'What the . . . ! I must be seeing things.' She could have sworn that she'd just watched a figure in a black cloak float towards the cemetery, then it had vanished.

With trembling fingers Angie grabbed hold of Sharon's arm, 'Did you see that?' she asked her voice trembling with fear.

'See what?' said Sharon annoyed with her friend as she didn't want to be distracted, she was happy just to look at all these Hallowe'en treats.

'That figure, the ghost in black,' added Angie. 'C'mon,' she said impatiently, 'we have to follow that ghost.'

'But I didn't see anything,' said Sharon. 'Your imagination is running away with you.' Now it was her turn to be whisked away.

The town hall clock chimed twelve as they walked arm in arm down the alley. There were no streetlights down here and the torch didn't help much either. Soon they'd reached the cemetery and as Angie opened the gates, she took a long look at the old derelict house opposite the graveyard. No one had lived in that place for years and years. It was rumoured to be haunted. The girls had just perched themselves on a bench when a sudden movement in the trees made Angie jump.

'What's that?' she asked all of a panic. 'Was it the wind?'

'I heard it too,' said Sharon in a whisper. 'Maybe it is your ghost after all.'

Although they couldn't see a thing, the rustling grew louder, Angie's stomach was doing somersaults.

'Let's hide in the old house, it can't be any scarier than this,' Sharon suggested.

Angie had to agree. The girls made a run for it down the path. In a flash they'd clambered over the rusty railings and into the garden. They stopped for a moment and shone the torch over the rubbish and decay. Old glass bottles, cans and newspapers littered the place, straggly weeds sat inside an old tyre. Then just as the girls were about to go inside, a chorus of blood-curdling screams pierced the air. The commotion was coming from inside the house. The screaming was quickly followed by a stampede of feet rushing down the stairs. The old wooden door was flung open and they watched in stunned silence as Wendy's gang rushed by them in a blur of speed before vanishing into the night. Without saying a word they took a deep breath and walked inside, coughing and spluttering as the dust swirled around them and clung to their clothes.

But the biggest surprise was still to come when they almost tripped over Wendy, who lay at the bottom of the stairs in an undignified heap. Both girls couldn't quite take it in, you could have heard a pin drop.

How humiliating, thought Angie, who was sorely tempted to leave her tormentor where she lay, but her conscience got the better of her.

As they helped her off the ground Wendy, now full of remorse, told them the following - 'We came here for a laugh, we were going to scare the hell out of you and Sharon 'cause I guessed you'd come here. Everyone knows about the rumours of this old house being haunted and to actually see a ghost on Hallowe'en as well as giving you a fright, that would have been so cool,' sighed Wendy, stopping for a moment before continuing. 'Everything was quiet until I opened the front door then all hell broke loose. Coming from somewhere upstairs was a very loud noise, like someone opening and shutting a door non-stop. Putting on a brave face but trembling with fear, I yelled up the stairs, 'Who's making that racket? We're coming to get you.' But the only reply was louder noises. I didn't want to investigate, I wanted to turn and run, but I'm the leader of the gang, I had no choice.

The stairs creaked and groaned as we made our way slowly upstairs. We crept along the landing towards the noise, I flung open the door and peered in. A very tall wardrobe in the corner of the room was the only piece of furniture and it was the wardrobe that was shaking and rattling. I got so scared and thought it might topple over at any minute. Anyway, the wardrobe doors bulged outwards like a balloon about to explode. So I crept closer and looked inside. What I saw chilled me to the bone. A very old man with wispy hair sat inside the wardrobe, he was covered in dust and cobwebs. He wore an old fashioned, crumpled suit and a trilby hat. By this time the gang had taken several steps back. We watched with baited breath as the old man stood up, raised his hat in greeting, stepped out of the wardrobe and disappeared before our very eyes! After several tense moments chaos returned. I started to scream, then the gang screamed too. I ran down those stairs as if my very life depended on it, with the gang in hot pursuit. In the panic that followed I got trampled and trod on. Those idiots didn't give a hoot about me. It was bedlam. I will never live this down. Wendy the Wimp, scared of a ghost. I shall be the laughing stock of the whole school.' At this horrible thought, Wendy burst into tears.

Angie listened with smug satisfaction, and she couldn't help thinking that ghost she'd caught sight of in the alley and the rustling in the trees of the cemetery had led her here to witness Wendy's downfall. *There was some kind of justice after all then!* though Angie with a smile.

As Angie and Sharon walked home arm in arm, Angie knew that she would never forget this Hallowe'en and how it had turned life around for the better. It would live inside her memory forever.

THE INTERVIEW
Pearl Cannon

Susan Blakey sat at her kitchen table, sipping a cup of strong tea. It was early, the sky just starting to lighten into pale pink and gold, and only the occasional chirp of a stirring bird disturbed the silence. Sleep had left her quite some time ago, and after restlessly tossing and turning for half an hour, she had swung her legs off the bed and had made her way to the kitchen. An interview later this morning with a prospective employer filled her mind as she anxiously anticipated possible answers to imagined questions. Emotionally she seemed to be on a roller-coaster ride - soaring with optimism one minute, in the depths of despair the next.

Susan's eyes wandered around her kitchen. Her home was warm and cheery and had always been filled with love and laughter - a safe haven from the cruel world outside. She had always enjoyed making it a good place for her husband to come home to. She and Geoff had enjoyed twenty-seven years of married bliss - truly a marriage made in Heaven. They had experienced their fair share of problems, but had always tried to overcome the obstacles together. They had no children and that cast a shadow over their lives for a time, but somehow they had come to terms with it and had focused rather on the blessings that they *did* have.

It was two years ago that Geoff had begun feeling off colour and had gone to see a doctor. The seriousness of the diagnosis and the realisation that they didn't have too much time left together came as a shock. The following months passed in a blur of hospitals, tests, and medication, with Susan hoping against hope, and finally saying goodbye. As she stood at the graveside, Susan realised that for the first time she was facing the future alone. It was a bleak prospect.

Geoff had begun his own little business in the early years of their marriage and together they had worked hard and the business had prospered. Although they had never considered themselves wealthy, they had been comfortable enough, making provision for their old age, putting a good bit away for emergencies, and doing what they could to make their lives financially secure. There was nothing left now. Just as the cancer had eaten away at Geoff's body, so too, the medical expenses had taken the nest egg that they had put aside. And still the bills had kept coming. Lying wide awake in her darkened bedroom in the early hours of countless mornings, Susan had calculated the outstanding debt, not knowing which way to turn.

She had taken charge of the administrative side of their business, keeping the books up to date in her organised way and making sure everything ran smoothly. She smiled to herself now, fondly remembering how Geoff would never charge the full price for those customers whom he knew were battling financially. 'Let's give them a bit of a discount, love,' he would say. He was always scrupulously honest with his customers - something she admired and with which she was in total agreement. There had never been a need or a desire to study further, to keep up to date with technology, and apart from the bit of computer work that she did for the business, she had no qualifications to speak of. This fact haunted her now. With very little money behind her, Susan was facing the prospect of finding a job in a world that had left her behind.

Over the past months she had scanned employment adverts, put her name down at several employment agencies and sent her CV in to numerous companies. Not one interview had been forthcoming. She realised she could never hope to compete with the younger set, and all their qualifications. They even spoke a different language! What did she know of RAMS and ROMS and all the computer jargon that people used these days? And with each rejection, she seemed to sink further and further into despair. She knew that she had something to offer the person who employed her. If she were given a chance to prove herself, she would show her employer that she could cope with responsibility. She was hardworking and efficient, and she was good with people. She would take night classes and get up to date with whatever computer courses were required. She was willing to learn - but how would any employer know this unless he first employed her? And who would want to employ someone who was over the hill and out of date? It just seemed like a vicious circle.

But yesterday, as she sat staring gloomily out of the window assessing her lot, the phone had rung. It was the manager of a local firm, calling to set up an interview with her for 10 o'clock this morning. She had seen the advert in the town's weekly paper and, although it was just a small company in a very seedy and dilapidated part of town, Susan applied anyway. She doubted that the salary would be much, but it was a start and she was in no position to be choosy. She needed a job desperately and so she would make the best of this interview. She would assure Mr Yardley, the manager, that she would be a willing, diligent and efficient employee who would go the extra mile. As the sun rose and flooded the kitchen with warmth and light, fifty-two year old Susan Blakey rinsed out her teacup and began planning what she would wear for the interview.

At 9.30 sharp, Susan stepped out of her front door and climbed into her green Toyota. She had allowed herself plenty of time so that she would arrive calm and composed. Humming to herself to overcome her nervousness, she backed into the street and set off towards town.

The main street was quiet, and Susan drove slowly, her thoughts on the forthcoming interview. Her last interview had been years ago - she had no idea what to expect. She could only be honest and hope for the best.

Ahead of her an elderly woman stepped off the sidewalk, intending to cross the road. What happened next was too quick for Susan's eye, but another glance in that direction showed her that the woman had fallen, her few parcels lying scattered around her on the edge of the road. Susan slowed down, edging to the kerb, wondering if someone would go to the old woman's aid, but no one else seemed to be nearby. The woman began to rise, but then sank down again, in obvious pain. Susan drove the Toyota into a parking bay and hurried over to see if she could assist, acutely aware of the precious minutes ticking by.

'Oh my dear, thank you for stopping. What a silly old woman I am! Tripping over my own feet!' the old lady exclaimed as she tried to rise the second time. Pain clouded her face, and when she put her weight onto her left foot, she sighed, 'It's no good dear, I can't walk. I think I've sprained my ankle.'

Susan looked around frantically for help, hoping that some Good Samaritan would take over and she could speed on to her interview. The few people around seemed to be hurrying towards their own destinations, intent on their own business, some giving her an apologetic smile, others just keeping their heads averted. 'Well, we'll have to get you home,' Susan replied, and backing her car closer to the injured woman, she helped her into the passenger seat.

Mrs Perkins' home was a neat little cottage on the outskirts of town. By the time Susan had her settled on the old fashioned couch in her lounge it was long past ten o'clock. She had insisted that someone be told of the old lady's predicament, and Mrs Perkins had reluctantly given her the telephone number of her son's office.

'We shouldn't bother Douglas, he's far too busy,' she pleaded, but Susan was adamant.

She was in the kitchen making the old lady a warm drink and dismally thinking that the slender chance of her getting a job had just gone down the drain, when she heard the front door open and a man's voice asked, 'Mother, are you alright? Why didn't you tell me you wanted to go into town?'

Mrs Perkins waved aside her son's concern and introduced Susan, explaining how Susan had helped her and brought her home.

Douglas Perkins was a large, kindly man with warm brown eyes and a relaxed manner. During the course of the conversation, Susan found herself opening up to him and telling him about her present situation. He listened carefully as she told of her husband's business and how they had worked as a team, the crushing illness and the medical bills and how daunting it was to find employment now that she was older.

A short while later, Susan climbed into her car and drove towards the industrial part of town. She was late for the interview now, but she hoped to see Mr Yardley anyway, and explain what had happened. She hoped that he would accept her excuse, though it sounded lame even to herself. On entering the small, grubby reception area, she explained who she was and why she was there, only to be told that Mr Yardley had just left for the city and would be away for a few days. 'I don't think it's worth rescheduling either,' the spiky-haired receptionist said, 'because Mr Yardley wanted someone to start immediately. Someone is starting tomorrow.'

Susan drove home. She unlocked the door, remembering how optimistic she had been when she had locked up just a few hours before. 'I did the right thing,' she said to herself. 'I could never have just driven past her lying on the side of the road, and if it means I have lost out on a job, well so be it!'

Later that evening as Susan was curled up in front of the TV, watching a comedy and trying to forget the events of the day, the phone rang. 'Hello, it's Douglas,' a cheery voice said. 'I wanted to know how you got on with your interview.'

'I didn't,' Susan replied, and proceeded to fill him in on what had happened.

'Well, I didn't want to mention anything until after your interview,' Douglas answered, 'but I have my own business which is doing well; at the moment my wife attends to the administrative side of it, but she would really like to spend more time on her drawing. She's an artist, you know. I have been looking around for someone dependable, who would be able to take care of things so that I can concentrate on the practical side of the business. What you did today made me realise that there are still people out there with good, old-fashioned values. It would be an honour to have you on my team. Would you consider it?' As he went on to discuss salary and benefits, Susan smiled to herself - the interview had been a success after all.

STEPPING STONES
T G Bloodworth

We both reached for the book at the same time. Our hands touched, startled, we both drew back, unbelieving at the source of the power we had both encountered. The public library is not exactly the place to meet new friends, however at that moment both of us were rather shaken.

I looked at her, trying hard not to stare, I found out later that it was a similar experience for her.

'My name's Helen,' she said once the initial shock had passed.

For me, two thousand ships had just launched! I'd been alone for some time now, often visiting the library for pleasure or just to be around people. This was the first time I'd actually 'met someone'.

We talked at length, oblivious of anyone else, of course she was a stranger in town, born and bred here, to me a new face stood out. Helen had come to visit a cousin, but arrived too late. Cousin Mary had passed away the day before she arrived. As we talked, I became more settled but still amazed at our encounter. It appeared that cousin Mary had lived just outside town, Helen was staying there for the moment. I asked her if I could walk her back, it was a long time since I had enjoyed conversation and good company. We wended our way slowly out of town. I remarked that I had often walked this way, years ago as a young lad we lived in a big house called 'Stepping Stones'.

Helen stopped for a moment, gathering her thoughts. 'What a coincidence,' she said, 'that's where I'm staying. It's cousin Mary's house. She had no family as such, having never married. I imagine when everything is sorted the house will be sold!'

As we approached 'Stepping Stones' I remembered how we had laughed and played as youngsters. The large orchard was no longer there, but some trees looked familiar. Entering by the front door, the red tiles greeted me, just for a moment I was lost in thought. The memories came flooding back, how happy I had been here. Even the parquet floor in the large living room was still in place. I smiled, recalling being told as a very young infant I had used them as building blocks.

Meanwhile Helen invited me to sit, refreshments were offered and we chatted. I told her all about my childhood, and recounted many stories from long ago.

Finally I said, 'It's time I was getting back.' I had encroached on her time and company for too long.

'Please don't rush away,' said Helen, 'I've no one else, I've really enjoyed being with you. Fate must have intended us to meet!'

'We could stay here together if you would like.'

'What about the new owners, do you think they would mind?' I asked.

'They will never know unless we make a nuisance of ourselves. Many buildings have ghosts, so what say you to two spirits taking up residence in 'Stepping Stones'?'

And that was how it was!

MOVING DAY
Julie Wealleans

It was a warm, sunny day and the seagulls circled overhead in the cloudless blue sky, uttering their familiar cries, the sound of which always reminded me of childhood seaside holidays. I was standing in the garden of a delightful cottage in Cornwall, viewing it as a prospective buyer. The cottage was set in a sleepy little seaside town with a pretty little harbour, where the tide lapped against the moored boats tethered by the Inn on the quay, and little cottages with gardens that looked out onto the sea, like the one I was viewing now. The breezy air was fresh and salty, carrying the aroma of the ocean, and of summer. At the bottom of the cottage garden, partially obliterating my view of the sparkling sapphire sea in the background behind it, was a very dilapidated wooden shed, with one window which was broken and dirty, with spider webs, moss and cobwebs clinging possessively to it. I just dismissed the old shed in my mind as another job to be done in the overgrown, unkempt garden, namely to take it down! I looked inside briefly, and apart from a few startled mice and abnormally large arachnids, there was nothing except a dusty shelf in there. All personal effects from the previous occupant had now been removed, except for a strange star-shaped symbol drawn on the wall. Knowing Cornwall to be a land steeped in legends of witchcraft and folklore, I recognised it as a pentacle, a witches' logo, and felt a shiver creep down my spine. I jumped as a freak draught suddenly shut the door behind me, and felt a sudden need to go back out into the summer sunshine, with the bumblebees and the smell of roses and honeysuckle. I hastily stepped back outside. Dismissing the moment as a remnant of my childish over-active imagination, I thought no more of it, as the over loquacious, unnaturally chirpy estate agent rambled on and on like the wild roses clambering up the far wall. I made a mental note to keep the roses, thinking them rather pretty, as I caught the occasional keyword or phrase from the estate agent's witterings. I learnt that the old lady who had lived there before had become unable to look after the garden, hence its state.

We went inside to view the very aesthetic little ivy-covered cottage, which by comparison, was spick and span, and beautifully kept. Again, all the previous occupant's possessions had gone, leaving a few basic items of furniture, which I mentally decided to replace with my own. It looked rather spartan and unloved, and I thought all it needed was a good spring clean, some carpets and curtains, and other homely touches. I turned to the estate agent, who was still verbalising nineteen to the dozen about exchanges of contracts and moving dates, and told her that I would like to make an offer on the cottage. A big smile beamed on her over-painted face and she immediately went into panic mode, scampering around in her smart suit, taking out her mobile phone and setting the conveyancing ball rolling before I could change my mind.

On moving-in day a few weeks later, an autumn Saturday, a close male friend of mine travelled down with me from my old home town and helped me move in. By late afternoon all my furniture and other possessions were in some semblance of order, and we were tired and hungry. He went out for Chinese food, and came back twenty minutes later, armed with two foil cartons containing piping hot, delicious smelling fare, and a chilled bottle of my favourite Zinfandel wine.

Half an hour later, we were sitting on the sofa watching an old movie, what was left of the take-away lying still uneaten on the coffee table, and we were laughing and talking nineteen to the dozen as usual. I don't know how it happened, I turned to look at him, smiling, ready to answer something he'd just said, and in that same split second, he reached forward to put down his drink or something. Anyway, it worked out that, quite by accident, his face was only inches away from mine when I looked round. I found myself gazing into his lovely blue eyes. He gazed back into mine, and we maintained eye contact for what seemed like an eternity. My heart was beating so loud, I felt sure he could hear it. Then I saw his gaze travel down to my mouth, and I knew at that second he was going to kiss me. I closed my eyes as his lips came down to mine, my heart going like an express train, and upon contact I felt a jolt of electricity so strong it took my breath away. He kissed me gently, tentatively. My arms slid up round his neck as he kissed me again, not so tentatively now he knew I wasn't going to push him away. Passion grew as our kissing became more urgent, and the movie on the television set faded into the distance as I snuggled into his arms. As he pushed me back on the sofa and his hands started grabbing at my clothes, my last coherent thought was that I was truly, madly and deeply under his spell.

Much later, I left him sleeping and busied myself clearing up the dinner things. The autumn sun was just setting as I gazed wistfully at it through the kitchen window. The beautiful hues of red, pink, blue, magenta, mauve, orange and gold in the sky resembled wispy paint strokes made by some celestial artist. Feeling in need of some air, I opened the window and stood looking out for ages, while the sky gradually turned navy blue, filled with a million glittering stars. It was a bit too breezy to stay there too long, and growing a little cold, I shut the window and decided to go to bed. I lay there lost in thought beside my sleeping companion for a while, like a love-struck schoolgirl, gazing at him and happily thinking about the events of the afternoon. I could hear the wind howling and an owl hooting outside, and in the distance I could hear the familiar rushing sound of the tide caressing the shore. By now, the cold silver moon was casting an eerie rippling reflection in the mirror on the wall opposite my bedroom window. My over-active imagination started up again as I thought I heard the creak of old wood in the garden, sounding like someone opening and shutting the shed door. The shed! I felt a twist of unease as I thought, for the first time since viewing the property back in the summer, about that shed and the momentarily chilling effect it had on me. That noise was just the shed door blowing in the wind, I decided, and resolving to buy a bolt for it the following day, I smiled a happy smile and settled down to sleep . . .

I was walking down the garden in my night-dress, and heading for the shed. Almost in slow motion, I saw my hand in front of me reach out to open the creaky door, and I stepped inside. Instead of an empty shed, I walked into a very strange scene. Over by the window was some sort of altar, covered by a purple velvet cloth stitched with gold, and bedecked with lighted candles of all colours. On the floor, like something out of a childhood story book, stood a huge, rusty black cauldron, with something bubbling away inside. It resembled apple sauce in colour and texture, but the smell was very different, like something dead and rotting. I crinkled up my nose and backed away from it. The shelf was littered with dirty jars containing various unlabelled items, which I did not wish to look at too closely. An old stained book lay on the rickety little table, open at a particular page. The picture closely resembled the contents of the bubbling and spitting cauldron on the floor. I picked up the book and studied the spell recipe set out on the page. Suddenly I was plunged into semi-darkness as the candles went out, and the shed became so cold it felt like below freezing. I dropped the book as I jumped in fright. My skin felt cold and clammy, and my breath came out in a vapour against the cold air. My heart hammered against my ribs like a terrified caged bird, as I looked around, shaking with terror. Suddenly I heard the chanting and cackling of several inhuman voices, as though some sort of ritual was going on around me, except I couldn't see anyone. All I could make out, from the milky moonlight seeping in through the dirty window, were ominous looking black shadows on every wall. They seemed to be coming closer and closer and the chanting got louder, and the shadows got bigger, and I tried with all my might to scream, but no sound would come out, just a pathetic inaudible whisper. The rational adult in me suddenly realised that I was simply having a nightmare, another result of my overactive imagination, and that any minute I'd wake up back in my bed in the cottage.

Minutes passed, however, and it dawned on me that the relief of a comforting awakening was not going to be forthcoming. I started to panic as the surreal, black, ectoplasmic presences around me got closer and closer as they approached through a floating spectral mist, so close I could hear the rustle of clothes. Then with a jolt of recognition, fear enveloped me like a thousand volts of electricity as I remembered the last ingredient on the spell recipe. The blood of one female adult . . .

INFORMATION

We hope you have enjoyed reading this book - and that you will continue to enjoy it in the coming years.

If you are interested in becoming a New Fiction author then drop us a line, or give us a call, and we'll send you a free information pack.

Alternatively if you would like to order further copies of this book or any of our other titles, then please give us a call or log onto our website at www.forwardpress.co.uk

New Fiction Information
Remus House
Coltsfoot Drive
Peterborough
PE2 9JX
(01733) 898101